When Marianne W
complaining that her parking lot is always full, she assumes it must be customers for the new restaurant next door. She's never met her neighbor, and with the parking lot situation, she has no interest in doing so. But when a snowstorm knocks out the power and traps both women in the building overnight, sparks fly—until the next morning, when the buried argument comes to a head.

Can they find a way to reclaim the magic of that night? And as decades-old secrets about the history of the town and Marianne's family come to light, can they work together to save both their businesses?

No Parking

Valentine Wheeler

A NineStar Press Publication

Published by NineStar Press
P.O. Box 91792,
Albuquerque, New Mexico, 87199 USA.
www.ninestarpress.com

No Parking

Printed in the USA
First Edition
February, 2020

Print ISBN: 978-1-951880-39-2

Also available in eBook, ISBN: 978-1-951880-40-8

Warning: This book contains sexually explicit content, which may only be suitable for mature readers.

For Thomas

Chapter One

The travel mug banged against the counter. Marianne jumped. "Jesus, Kevin! I didn't hear you come in."

"It's full again." Kevin crossed his arms and glared. "The parking lot back there." He made a show of glancing around the nearly empty bakery, eyes pausing on Zeke in the corner, mug in his hands and laptop open as usual, big red headphones covering his ears. He crossed his arms. "Why do you pay that kid if all he does is ignore you? And the customers?"

"You're in a mood this morning." Marianne pushed herself off the stool and grabbed his aluminum coffee mug. Her ex-husband was still an attractive man fifteen years after their divorce, and she couldn't work up the energy to be annoyed at him for it anymore. "If you want to go next door and complain about the cars, go ahead." She filled his mug with hazelnut coffee, added an espresso shot, capped it, and handed it back. "It's not like our customers are beating down the doors for spots right now."

"I did go next door," Kevin grumbled, taking the cup. "It wasn't productive." Now it was him avoiding her gaze.

The parking lot issue wasn't a new one—it had been a problem for a few months—and on a busy day Marianne would be filled with a low-level simmering rage as customer after customer complained about it. Still, she wasn't going to tell Kevin that. Their relationship had improved in the years since their divorce but not quite that much.

"Not productive?" she pressed.

He sipped his coffee to cover the slight flush in his pale cheeks and didn't answer.

"She threw you out, didn't she?" Marianne's estimation of her neighbor and nemesis rose a notch. "You tried to yell at her, and she didn't take it."

"I was very polite!"

"Hm." Marianne put her hands on her hips and considered the man she'd spent nearly twenty-five years married to. He could be charming when he wanted to be—the whole silver fox, sparkling blue eyes and white teeth politician thing—though he never tried it with her anymore. Many women had found him suave and attractive during their marriage and probably still did. But when he wanted something from someone with no interest in what he was peddling? Politeness wasn't his style. Generally, once charm had failed, he whined worse than any of their three kids had as toddlers. She'd learned that plenty during their marriage, and again during the divorce. "I'm sure you were."

"I can talk to Bruce and Andrea," said Kevin. "Just because I'm retired—"

"No need to get the city council involved, Kevin. I'll handle my own property, thanks." She glanced at the clock on the wall, its tarnished brass pendulum swinging below the cracked glass. "Aren't you going to be late for your train?" He was still showing up at transit meetings in the city every other week since he had been appointed to the regional transit board as community representative now that he wasn't an elected official. Kevin had a habit of holding onto things too tightly and refusing to let them go.

Kevin glanced down at his watch and swore. "Yeah. Shit." He took another long gulp of coffee and leaned over the counter to kiss Marianne's cheek. "Thanks. Who knew retirement could be so busy?" He turned to hurry out the door and then stopped and glanced back over his shoulder. "You be good, all right? Don't work too hard."

Marianne rolled her eyes and shooed him out with a towel.

*

It wasn't that she didn't notice the number of customer complaints about the parking lot. Every third customer mentioned it, even the ones who took the train in or walked. She supposed in her great-grandfather's day when the bakery had had a dozen employees and filled the entire building, it hadn't been a problem. The old rail for parking—well, tying, technically—horses was still there, a deeply worn set of posts by the dumpster. In 1892, no one had complained about the lack of space for cars. They'd been more worried about whose sheep had wandered into whose pasture.

Of course, Marianne wouldn't have been running things back then. And even if she had been allowed to work, she'd probably be in petticoats or some other kind of nonsense. She'd take the complaints in exchange for being able to wear jeans to work and the right to vote. And maybe once the winter snows really started up, she could convince Ray to do a less-than-perfect plowing job. That would show that woman next door. See how she liked the constant complaints.

Feeling a little better, if a little petty, she pulled a tray of cranberry muffins from the oven, their tops steaming and barely cracked, glistening with sugar crystals, as the bell over the door chimed. She smiled at the thin black man who shuffled in. "Hey, there, Joe," she called. "Eight o'clock already?"

Zeke glanced up and pulled his headphones off, shutting his computer. "Hey, Grandpa!"

"Ezekiel, Ms. Windmere." He nodded at them each solemnly. "A beautiful morning out there. Though I hear the sunlight isn't going to last."

Zeke helped him to a seat, a hand hovering under his elbow. Joe shooed him away, then pulled his rolled newspaper from his back pocket and smoothed it on the table with gnarled hands.

"Your usual?" asked Marianne. Joe Mitchell was one of many reasons she'd never fire Zeke for taking breaks as long as he wanted a job. Ninety-eight years old and still living on his own, Joe had been a delivery boy for her great-grandfather in the thirties before they both went to war. He was family. And he remembered Windmere Bakery in its heyday. Most importantly, he walked, and since it was around the back, he'd never once asked about the parking lot.

"I saw Ms. Wahbi this morning," he said as he accepted a cinnamon scone, already toasted and buttered. He breathed in appreciatively, savoring the spiced steam rising from its crisp top. "That's the longest anyone's lasted in the building in years."

"It's only been a few months," said Zeke. "There's really been nobody who stayed that long? What, is the place haunted or something?"

Joe leaned forward, cane tapping the floor by Zeke's foot. "We don't like to talk about it, Ezekiel, but there was an accident back in 1979—"

Marianne suppressed a snort of laughter as Zeke leaned forward, eyes wide in his brown face. "An accident?"

"It was a paper business back then, with huge cutting machines that sliced the reams to size, and one night, late in September, a young man was working late. He shouldn't have been there after-hours. Told his boss he'd finished something he hadn't. He wasn't paying attention—he was listening to some record instead of watching his fingers—and the next morning they found his arm in a case of paper. Donna Summer was still playing on the record player." His cracked voice lowered as he paused to chew his scone. "Sometimes, in the evening, you'll still hear the strains of MacArthur Park playing through the wall."

"Really?"

Joe whacked Zeke in the knee with his newspaper. "No, boy. Don't be a fool. There's no such thing as ghosts." He finished the last bite and winked.

Zeke stared at him, betrayed, as Marianne suppressed a snort. Joe grinned at her and pushed himself upright. He tucked his coffee into the cupholder of his walker and pressed bills into Marianne's hand. "You take care of that idiot grandson of mine, Ms. Marianne." Still shaking his head, he patted her on the shoulder as he passed and then clapped Zeke fondly on the back before shuffling out the door.

Zeke waited until the door closed behind his great-grandfather, a smile fighting its way onto his face and then turned to Marianne. "No customers yet, huh?"

"What do you mean? We had Kevin, and Joe—"

"No *paying* customers yet. Grampa and your ex don't count."

"Kevin pays! I consider it his alimony." Marianne glanced up at the clock. "It is a little odd, I guess. But it's still early. The lunch rush won't start for another few hours."

As she spoke, the door swung open, the bell over it jingling loudly. A familiar figure in navy blue strolled in, her short dark hair tousled by the winter wind and the tip of her usually brown nose reddened with cold. She let the door swing shut behind her and leaned on the counter.

"Doris! Anything good in the mail for us today?"

Doris pushed back the brim of her postal cap and smiled. "Hey there, Marianne, Ezekiel. Just the two of you this morning?" She flipped through the pile of letters in her arms and then pulled a manila envelope from her satchel. "Would have thought you'd be mobbed the way the cars are out there. You can have this if you've got one of those almond croissants saved for me. You're the only place I know who do those toasted salty almond slivers on top, you know? Can't find them anywhere else."

Zeke laughed, his cheeks a little darker as he smiled up at their tall, gorgeous mail lady. "And you won't find them anywhere else, ma'am. They're a Windmere Bakery specialty. I'll get you one."

Marianne watched him hurry behind the counter and leaned in toward Doris. "He knows you're married, right?"

"Considering Tasha was his math teacher last year, I should hope so," replied Doris, voice low. "It's sweet though. And he's a good kid."

"He spent a lot of time doing homework for their class," mused Marianne. "Maybe he's got it bad for both of you."

"Coffee?" called Zeke from the pastry case.

"Yes, please," Doris raised her voice. "Milk, one sugar. Thanks, kiddo." She pulled out her wallet and handed Marianne a ten. "Hey, give the kid the change. Might make his day." She set their mail down on a table and took her coffee and pastry bag from a blushing Zeke at the counter. "Have a good day, folks."

Business picked up after that—locals and regulars trickling in and slowly filling up the eight tiny tables that crammed the small area between the counter and the wall. Carol Ramirez stopped by to buy three-dozen chocolate-chip cookies to sober up late-night drunken bar customers, dropping off a gallon of fresh homebrew for Marianne's beer bread experiments, and Sheri Ng picked up a whole tray of muffins for some kind of board meeting at the new office park. Marianne and Zeke stayed busy as the sky darkened outside the wide glass windows.

Ray Bell stomped in around two thirty, with Fatima, one of the admins at the high school, hands pausing their signed conversation as they entered. Ray called a hello to Zeke, unbuttoning his coat and hanging it over a chair, as Fatima considered the pastry case. "Getting cloudy out there," Ray observed. "What do you think, Marianne? This gonna be the big one this year?"

Marianne smiled. "I'm always wrong about the weather, Ray." She waved at Fatima, who waved back and pulled out her phone. Marianne did the same, once again making a mental note to try to learn more sign language. She'd known Fatima nearly forty years, since her family had settled in Swanley so her father could commute to his grad school program in Boston. About Marianne's height, Fatima was slender where Marianne was broad. She and Ray, six feet tall and a former linebacker at Swanley High, made an odd but familiar sight. But the two of them had been close friends since high school.

Channel Five says at least six inches tonight, Fatima texted. *Are you staying open?*

Marianne nodded, making sure Fatima was looking her way before she spoke. "For a while. I don't have far to go."

"Hoping we don't lose power again this time," said Ray, accepting the coffee Marianne handed him. "Last time it was three days till we got it back. A cold three days. The wife made me buy a generator the day Harvey's opened back up. I swear that hardware store takes half my paycheck with how often I'm in there."

Marianne shivered. "I keep meaning to get a generator or something, but I only remember when it's too late."

Fatima tapped the glass, pointing at a chocolate croissant. *And a coffee,* she texted. *Black, please. The Starbucks in Wilshire closed already. You may get a rush.*

"Wimps." Marianne put the croissant on a plate and took Fatima's card, swiping it through the reader.

How are the kids? Fatima asked.

"They're good," said Marianne. "Janie's finished her program and started working as a nurse out in Detroit. Jacob's heading back to school in the fall in California. Anna's working as an architect in Pittsburgh." She passed Fatima her food and drink. "I know Janie's coming back next year for her ten-year reunion at the high school."

Fatima smiled. *I'll see her then.* She signed the receipt and settled down across from Ray.

By the time late afternoon rolled around, Zeke was long gone, and Marianne was happy to see the last customer of the afternoon rush out the door, leaving her alone in an empty bakery. She glanced at the pile of trays to be washed, the dusting of flour across the surfaces, the muddy patch in front of the door where snow boots had dragged in half a town's worth of dirt, and then she slumped down in a chair, taking a moment to rest. She needed a vacation. She needed a *retirement*.

The first few flakes were beginning to fall outside now, the low heavy clouds promising to worsen the precipitation before long. Marianne didn't mind the snow. Not really, not until slush sat gray and wet in the gutters for weeks at a time. That's when she longed to be anywhere but the town where she'd spent nearly all her sixty years.

Zeke's main complaint, on the other hand, had been that snow on a Saturday wouldn't give him any break from his classes. She'd countered that most of his classes were online, anyway, so he had no excuse. If they'd had online classes when she'd been in school, she might have finished more quickly and done better afterward. Maybe she'd be off somewhere in a high-powered job, planning her three-week vacation in Aruba right now, instead of scrubbing hard-baked chocolate off a metal tray that had seen better days.

Thinking of Zeke reminded her of her own kids—she'd told Janie, her middle kid, that she'd give her a call over the weekend. Given the way the weather was looking, she figured it would be better to call sooner rather than later. She started what parts of closing she could, bagging the leftover savory pastries to make into croutons and the sweet ones to munch on herself later since she wasn't going to make it out to the shelter to donate them before they went stale.

The various doughs and batters for the morning she prepped as much as she could, premixing huge batches of flour and sugar and baking soda and salt into various proportions to add liquid to in the morning, and sticking tubs of muffin batter in the fridge beside buckets of diced berries and chocolate and nuts. She even gave the old monster of a gas stove a good scrub down, working the cast iron until the dark metal gleamed.

She noticed as she stacked trays covered in plastic wrap that her prepped macarons were running low: she'd have to plan a long day of mixing and piping in the next week or two to build up a buffer of chocolate, lavender, and green tea for the next month's specials. She was especially proud of the lavender—she'd seen someone make them on a cooking show, and the idea had gripped her for weeks before she'd figured out the recipe. Now, they were one of her biggest sellers when they appeared on the specials list.

Marianne glanced at the laminated list on the wall beside the entrance to the pantry, reading under her breath through the familiar instructions. Some things had changed in the nearly sixty years since her grandfather had turned the bakery over to her father—the nighttime cleaning instructions weren't one of those things. Daniel Windmere Senior's familiar handwriting, slanted and neat, still led her through the tasks she could probably do in her sleep. She read the list every evening the bakery was open, and she would keep doing so until whichever of her kids she could bribe into taking over let her slide into a graceful retirement somewhere far away. Somewhere warm. Hawaii. Arizona. Anywhere but rural Massachusetts, with its changeable weather, its small-town gossip, and its neighbors who didn't understand how to share a damn parking lot.

The snow was falling faster out the big glass window now, starting to stick in a quickly thickening layer on the sidewalk. Marianne leaned against the counter, watching the few people still outside fighting against the wind. None of them looked like they were interested in croissants.

She shook her head and pushed herself upright to flip the sign on the door to Closed and turned the deadbolt. It was nights like these that made her glad she'd moved back into the apartment above the shop.

"I'd probably get hit by a car in all this snow," she muttered. "I'm stuck in here till the plows come through." She had plenty of food and supplies between the shop and the apartment. She hardly left the building most days, anyway. Most of her necessities were delivered to the shop, and she could get anything else on her weekly grocery store run. Her kids had wanted her to find someplace new when she'd sold the house. They'd said it wasn't healthy for her to move back where she worked, especially when she could afford to buy something small in a nearby neighborhood with the revenue from the sale.

Janie especially had objected, saying Marianne would end up even more isolated and lonely. Marianne had scoffed and reminded them she'd grown up in the apartment back when her grandfather had been the one running things, and she'd been living there when she'd met their father, so how isolating could it be? Besides, she'd used the money from the old house to pay Anna's tuition, so she really shouldn't complain. She didn't need to be investing in new real estate at her age. And the apartment was nice and toasty—

The lights flickered. Marianne flinched and pushed open the door to her apartment in the back of the kitchen, climbing the narrow rickety stairs. The ovens had been burning since four a.m., trays and trays of croissants and muffins and pies that had flown off the shelves until a few moments after the first flakes had fallen. Even if the power went out, the heat from the day's baking would linger for a few hours at least. For the hundredth time, she wished she'd gotten around to installing the backup generator or switching to gas. Electric heat sounded great until the power went out. She supposed she could start baking to raise the temperature, but the idea of messing with knives and fire in the dark didn't appeal. Besides, her body ached. She'd spent her day in and out of ovens and fridges. The last thing she wanted to do now was bake more.

The living room was dark and a little chilly, so she cranked the thermostat up to seventy-three. Might as well get a little extra heat in the apartment while she could, knowing the state of the power grid. Deep within the walls, the heat clicked on, whirring to life. She rummaged in the counter drawer nearest the door until she found the box of emergency candles, and the big green safety flashlight Kevin had gotten her for Christmas one year. Theoretically, it glowed in the dark, but not if she kept it in a dark drawer all the time. She also pulled a few logs from the rack beside the fireplace, settling them in the iron grate and stuffing newspaper and twigs into the space below.

Another gust of wind rattled the windows. Marianne shivered. Was that thunder?

A crack of wind shuddered the building. The branches of the old pine tree out front scraped against the windows. A groan outside signaled the fall of snow against the power lines, and the lights flickered again before sputtering out. With a slow groan, the heat pump stuttered and then stopped.

Marianne let out the breath she'd been holding. The dark was familiar. In the dark, with the sound of snow and wind against the windows in the air, the apartment could be fifty years in the past. With her eyes closed, her grandfather could be around the corner in the master bedroom, her father and mother in the spare room, her cousins stuffed into bunk beds in the warm little office above the bakery stove. The quiet inside broke the illusion though. Even with no one awake, the apartment had felt full, breaths and creaks and stifled giggles and cries. Even in a storm, it was louder inside than out. Now it was empty except for her.

She picked up a candle from the kitchen counter and searched around for matches. None in the junk drawer, and none above the mantle where they should be. Where—

Marianne groaned, remembering the birthday party they'd hosted earlier in the week. She'd borrowed the matches from the apartment for it, and she'd probably left them downstairs next to the cake case. It had been a lovely party, even though most of the guests had had to park in the municipal lot a block and a half away since the parking lot had been completely full of customers for the Cairo Grill next door.

Outside, the last streetlight fizzled out, leaving a blackness outside the window broken only by the distant glow from the battery-powered lights of the train station. On the table, the flashlight's body glowed the faintest shade of green, and Marianne stumbled to it. Its beam wasn't very bright once she flicked the switch on, but the faint light was enough to get her back to the staircase without breaking her neck. She made her way carefully to the bottom, found the matches right where she'd left them, and shook her head at her own folly. She pulled one out and struck it to light one of the candles she used for events and then tucked the box into her apron pocket.

Flashlight in one hand, candle in the other, she wended her way back through the furniture to the stairs. Not trusting the thin, wavering light, she slid a foot out until she tapped the stair's riser with her toes and worked her way carefully up to the landing and then around the turn. Then a stair wasn't quite where she expected, and she gasped, dropping flashlight and candle. She grabbed for the rail, slipping and landing with a thud on her rear, barely avoiding knocking her face into the bannister. She groaned and tried to lever herself back upright without falling any farther and then slid on her butt down the remaining steps. She stopped at the bottom, breathing heavily, and fumbled for the flashlight that still glowed faintly on the floor a few feet away. The candle, thank goodness, had gone out when it landed. She didn't love the idea of trying to reach the fire department in the middle of a snowstorm.

A sound filtered through the wall. She froze and listened carefully, heart pounding in her throat.

"Hello?" called the voice again, faint through the wood and plaster. "Is everything all right?"

"Who's there?"

A pause. "Rana. Rana Wahbi," said her neighbor. "Ms. Windmere? Is that you?"

Marianne pushed herself upright and then froze as her ankle twinged when she put her weight on it. She gasped aloud, squeezing her eyes shut as she hopped on the other foot.

"Ms. Windmere?" The woman's voice was pleasant and concerned, lightly accented, and low-pitched. "Are you all right?"

Could that really be the woman who'd been keeping all Marianne's customers away for months with her parked cars? Nearly three months they'd worked on opposite sides of the building, Marianne realized, and this was the first time they'd spoken. She sounded nice. That was the strangest part. "I'm fine," she called back.

"Are you sure? That was quite a crash. Did something fall?"

"Just me. I slipped and twisted my ankle, I think."

There was a pause through the wall, long enough that Marianne wondered if Ms. Wahbi left.

Marianne pressed her fingers to the side of her ankle, feeling for a bump or blood or something.

"Do you need help?"

Was her parking lot nemesis really offering *help*?

"I'm fine," she said. "Just need to rest for a minute." She tried the ankle again and winced. *Stupid*, she thought. *Stupid to be here alone, stupid to leave the matches downstairs when I knew there was a storm coming, and stupid to let my pride overwhelm my common sense. Maybe the girls were right. Maybe I'm old and frail and not safe living by myself.* "This is exactly what my kids warned me about."

"What's that?"

"They told me if I lived alone here, I might fall and hurt myself, and no one would find me. That I need to, as Janie put it, be 'aware of my changing body.' I think it was revenge for my puberty talk twenty years ago."

Ms. Wahbi laughed. "You're not exactly decrepit," she said. "Do they think you're that old?"

"I'm not sure," Marianne admitted. "Janie—my middle girl—she's a nurse. She's always fussing."

"Well, if you called loudly enough, I would hear when I came in to start the marinades. So, you wouldn't lay there more than a day—or two, if you fell on a Monday."

"That's reassuring. I'm closed Mondays, too, so at least that's unlikely." She tested the ankle again. Still a little sore, but much better. Good. That meant it probably wasn't sprained, only tender. She pulled her robe closer around herself, shivering in the stairwell as the heat continued to leach from the drafty old building now that the power was out. The silence drew out longer, and she wondered if the other woman had moved elsewhere.

She didn't even know why she was talking to her, except that the dark chilly stairs with the faint sound of snow pattering on the roof and windows was an odd sort of magical, liminal place where a disembodied voice seemed to fit right in. The fact that this woman had been a source of ire recently didn't seem to matter when the wind whistled through the trees outside, and the shadows stood tall and ghostly. Still, she cleared her throat and tried to pull herself together.

"It must be getting cold over there," said Ms. Wahbi. "I've made tea on the stove if you'd like some. At least the gas is still on." Her voice was cautious as if she knew Marianne wasn't likely to accept.

"No, thank you," said Marianne. "I'm just getting a few things and settling in upstairs." She wasn't about to get murdered in the dark over a parking lot dispute. If the woman next door had cursed Marianne as much as Marianne had her, she couldn't imagine that would be a good idea.

"You live above the bakery?"

"I do," said Marianne. "I'm going to ride out the storm up there. Thanks for your concern." She tried to make her tone sound final. Then she pulled out a fresh match and lit the candle once more, the guttering, sputtering sound of the wick catching loud in the near silence.

"Good luck," said Ms. Wahbi. "I'm hoping there's enough of a break in the storm I can make it home. I may have power there."

Marianne felt her mothering instincts kick in automatically. "Driving? In this weather?" she burst out.

"Well, with no heat, I don't think I'll stay here in the restaurant."

"Still." Marianne tested the ankle again, resting her full weight on it this time. It seemed all right. She felt strange, leaning here against the wall, hands cupped around the candle as the wick steadied, speaking with the woman she'd been silently cursing for three months.

"May I ask a favor?" Ms. Wahbi's voice was quiet through the drywall.

Marianne had the slightest moment of hesitation. What favor could this neighbor, this stranger, want from her? The whole lot? The sidewalk out front, maybe?

"Could I perhaps borrow your phone? I need to call my son back and let him know I'm all right. We were in the middle of a conversation when the power went out, and my cell phone is out of battery."

"Of course," said Marianne. "I was about to call my daughter. You'll have to come around though. There's no way through the building."

"I think I can manage that much," said Ms. Wahbi. "The front door? And it won't be too much trouble, with your ankle, to come let me in?"

"It's fine," said Marianne. "I'm not the one walking through a blizzard." She pushed herself upright. "You know where to go?"

Ms. Wahbi laughed. "Yes, I do. I drive past your door every morning."

Marianne knew she did. She saw her silver Outback come around the building most mornings around nine and simmered, knowing it was likely to pull into the last available spot in the lot.

A rustling sounded from the other side of the wall. "All right," Ms. Wahbi said. "I'll see you in a few minutes."

Chapter Two

Marianne limped her way back carefully through the darkened kitchen to the store's door, trying not to put too much pressure on her sore ankle. She gave up on the flashlight as she hobbled through the customer seating to the broad wooden door that had marked the public entrance to her family's bakery for the last century and a half. She set the candle down on Zeke's table and stared out the steamy old glass pane, trying to see if she could discern any movement outside. The street was dark; the flickering of the candle occasionally illuminating a few swirling flakes, but not much else.

She hoped Zeke and Joe were home safe, warm in their little house down the road, and that they had power. Joe's house was even older than the bakery, dating back to the mid-1700s. The first floor had a working wood stove that, in a pinch, could heat Joe's bedroom and the living room. She hoped Zeke had the sense to sleep in the living room if his room was too cold.

She worried about that kid. Ever since the troubles with his parents when he was fourteen—when he'd told them he was a boy—he'd been living with Joe. And while Joe was hale for his nineties, he was beginning to slow down physically. Zeke had begun doing more and more for him as the last year had gone on. Marianne supposed, in the end, they each benefitted from having the other around the way family should even if theirs was an unconventional situation. She hoped nothing went wrong while the streets were so impassable. And if something did happen, she hoped Zeke's mother—Joe's granddaughter, and their only local relative—got over herself enough to come over and help. She only lived six blocks away, but she hadn't visited since Zeke changed his name and moved in with Joe.

She pulled a chair over to the door and tucked her robe closer around herself. The thought occurred to her that she would be meeting her neighbor for the first time in her blue flannel jammies.

Still no sign of Ms. Wahbi outside. Marianne got up from the chair to stare out again, cupping her fingers around her eyes and squinting. Her breath fogged the cold glass, and her stomach soured with the tiniest burn of worry. She had just begun considering whether she should get her snow boots to go out and search when something moved outside.

She hoped the movement was Ms. Wahbi. Better her than a lost angry bear or something. As that thought crossed her mind, she realized that apart from a very general image of a Middle Eastern woman approximately her own age, she didn't actually know what Ms. Wahbi looked like. That was sad, somehow.

The movement resolved into a vaguely human-shaped smear against the gray swirling wind and then into a woman wrapped tightly in a parka, mittens, hat, and boots. Marianne hurried to open the door and usher her inside and then closed it tightly behind her. Even the few seconds the door had been open had left a scattering of wet white snow ten feet into the store and had dropped the temperature another few degrees. "You made it," she said as the woman pulled off her hood with shaking hands, revealing a face about Marianne's age with round cheeks, luminous brown eyes, and soft waves of chestnut brown hair.

"I followed the wall the whole way around," she said, her accent more pronounced when not muffled by six inches of wall. "I nearly fell into the hedge." She shivered. "I wasn't sure I was going to make it. Visibility is absolutely nothing out there. Not a soul on the roads, thank goodness." White flakes of snow speckled her thick dark hair cascading around her shoulders, a flush darkening the apples of her cheeks as she shook herself and caught her breath. She stood a few inches shorter than Marianne with fine lines around her eyes and a few gray hairs at her temples.

"Here," said Marianne, taking her coat and draping it over a chair to let the snow slide loose. Ms. Wahbi wore a thick sweater beneath it, and her soft-looking silk pants were shoved into knee-high Wellingtons that didn't look quite snow-appropriate. They looked more like something a fisherman would wear to wade in summer surf, not warm enough for this weather. "Let me find my phone."

She kept an old flip phone down here to use in emergencies like this one, or to lend out to visiting friends and family. Luckily, it was plugged in exactly where she'd left it that evening, nearly fully charged. She pulled the phone from the charger and handed it to Ms. Wahbi. "Here, you can call your son back."

"Thank you again," her neighbor replied, taking the phone. "And I don't think we've ever been introduced. It's good to finally meet you. Please call me Rana."

"Marianne." Marianne smiled awkwardly. "You can borrow the phone if you'd like. And my number is the only contact in there, if you need to get in touch."

"I brought you a gift," said Rana. "It's not much, but I wanted to give you a taste of my restaurant." She pulled out a pastry bag from the outer pocket of her coat, slightly squashed. "To thank you for the use of your phone."

"That wasn't necessary," said Marianne, but she took the bag.

Rana stomped her feet on the mat, shaking the slush loose from her boots. "I'll try not to damage your hedge any further on my way back," she said.

Marianne felt her own mother's voice rising in her chest, the hospitality their Greek family had held sacred. She fought against it for a few long seconds and then finally said, "Would you like to come upstairs? You can make your call there. It's probably warmer than in your store and more comfortable than down here."

Rana gave her a long, considering look, suspicion on her face warring with what Marianne assumed was the thought of shivering in the dark, damp bakery any longer. "That's very kind," she said finally. "Let me call my Amir back from here and then perhaps if the storm hasn't gotten any better. Thank you." Her eyes didn't leave Marianne's, looking for something in Marianne's gaze.

Marianne felt herself blush. She didn't usually invite strangers up to her apartment. And she wasn't sure why she was so easily letting go of her annoyance at the woman—but somehow it didn't seem right, now that they were face-to-face, and Rana was cold and snow damp. Besides, she'd always had a weakness for a pretty face. That was one reason she and Kevin had stayed married as long as they had: she liked looking at him, and it weakened her resolve. Making a silent pledge not to let Rana's long eyelashes do any more damage, Marianne did a mental inventory, trying to remember if she'd left any messes around the apartment.

She busied herself in the kitchen behind the bakery finding more candles and opening the refrigerator quickly to pull out the things that were most likely to go bad if the electricity wasn't restored—although, if the temperature inside kept dropping, the fridge might be warmer than the surrounding room by tomorrow evening. From the front, she could barely hear the muffled strains of Ms. Wahbi—Rana, she reminded herself—speaking in another language, soothingly, into the phone. Arabic, maybe? Rana was from Egypt, if she remembered correctly. She was embarrassed to realize she wasn't even sure if that's what they spoke in Egypt. It was, wasn't it? She knew people always thought Fatima spoke Arabic, despite being from Pakistan, and the error annoyed the heck out of the whole Siddiqui family. Marianne didn't want to make the same mistake with Rana.

Finally, she heard the jingle of the bell over the door and then a thud as it closed again. Had she left just like that?

Rana reappeared, the front of her jacket dripping with snow. "I think I may take you up on your kind offer," she said. "I'm so sorry to impose."

Marianne smiled. "That's all right." She hefted the bag she'd filled. "I need someone to help me eat the food that would be going bad down here, anyway."

"If you're sure…"

"Come on," said Marianne. "You can keep me company while we're snowed in."

Rana nodded, face breaking into a smile that showed slightly crooked teeth and the depth of her relief. "All right." *She has a beautiful smile*, Marianne thought, forcing herself to look away. *I'm in trouble.*

As they climbed the stairs, Marianne was suddenly very aware of how drab and bare the apartment was. Ever since moving back in ten years earlier, she'd meant to decorate and pull some more of the old heirloom furniture out of storage. And every year she didn't do it. So, the apartment had nothing but the battered old furniture they'd left for the renters with a few personal touches. She hadn't thought of what it might look like to a stranger.

"Just through here." She closed the door behind Rana, shivering a little. The air in the apartment had cooled considerably. She was glad Anna and Jacob had put plastic over her windows at Thanksgiving. The extra insulation would keep the heat in a little bit longer. "So, why didn't you go home before the storm hit?" she asked as she began stacking kindling and newspaper in the fireplace. "This isn't a great night to be stuck out and about."

Rana laughed a little. "I meant to go home, but customers kept coming in and wanting takeout. Besides, I didn't think it was going to get so bad so quickly."

"Still not used to Massachusetts winters?" She lit a match and smiled in satisfaction as the flames caught on the crumpled newspaper below the fireplace grate and then flipped the damper open. She shivered as a blast of cold air nearly extinguished the fledgling flames.

"I suppose not." She glanced out the window at the swirling gray. "I've been here fifteen years, and winter still surprises me every year." She shook her head. "On nights like this one, I wonder if I should have stayed in Charleston. Though it is pretty out there."

"Why'd you come up north?" asked Marianne, curious. "You're Egyptian, right? I'm thinking the climate down south is more what you're used to."

"It is," admitted Rana. "But I had a friend in Boston. She let us stay with her for a few months when we first arrived, before we settled in Charleston. I loved the area, so when all my children moved out, I came back."

"You have more than the one son?"

"Oh yes," said Rana. "My daughter Nour is my oldest, then Amir, then my twins Samia and Sayed. Can I help with the fire?"

Marianne stacked a pair of logs on the grate. "That's all right. I've got a process. Former Girl Scout." She sat back on her heels as the kindling crackled. "Are they nearby, your kids?"

"No. Samia and Amir are in California. Nour and Sayed are in Cairo, in Egypt."

"My son Jacob is in California too," said Marianne, setting the bag of perishables from downstairs on the counter by the window where the air was coldest. "Berkeley. I can't imagine having him any farther. My other two are in Pittsburgh and Detroit, so they're a little closer. And they're near enough to each other just in case."

"I'm glad my children are in pairs, at least," said Rana. "Nour offered to let Sayed stay with her while he studied," she said. "I don't see them as often as I would like."

"Me either," said Marianne. "And Anna calls me, but the other two? I have to hunt them down for a ten-minute update."

"My boys are like that," Rana sighed. "I miss them on nights like this especially. This has been harder than I expected it to be, running this business without them to help. I've always had at least my twins to wait tables."

"None of my kids wanted anything to do with the bakery," admitted Marianne. "I thought one of them might someday, but it isn't looking good." She glanced up at the ceiling. "I don't know what'll happen to this place when I'm gone."

"I'm sure nothing else Mr. Leventi put in would be as lovely as your bakery," said Rana.

Marianne stared at her. "Mr. Leventi? He'll own this place over my dead body."

"He isn't your landlord?"

Marianne bristled. "Absolutely not." She waved at the building around them. "The Windmere family has owned this building since we built it in 1866."

"Even my restaurant?"

"My father had to sell part of the building back in the sixties," Marianne admitted grudgingly. "But yes, even that."

"I'm glad you still own your bakery," said Rana. "Mr. Leventi has not been the easiest landlord to have. Especially not now that he's running for office."

"I've heard," said Marianne. "Most businesses don't last long in that space. I'm amazed yours seems to be thriving despite that." The temperature was really starting to drop, even in the warmth of the room above the oven. Rana shivered, tucking her hands inside the sleeves of her shirt. Marianne reached behind the couch and pulled out a few blankets, draping one over Rana. "Here," she said. "You look cold." She wrapped herself in the other and set a tray beside the fire, pouring marinara in a bowl near the flames and setting a loaf of bread to warm. "Does this need to be heated?" She held up the bag Rana had brought her.

"It wouldn't hurt," replied Rana. "It's only a few cheese turnovers, and they're good either way."

Marianne opened the bag, letting out a waft of a delicious savory scent, and arranged them beside the bread next to the fire.

"Have you ever considered switching from electric heat?" asked Rana. "Then you wouldn't be in this bind." She smiled, dark brown eyes twinkling. "Although the fire is helping. As is the company."

"No room for an oil tank," Marianne said, pulling the blanket tighter around herself and settling back on the couch. "And the gas lines aren't the most reliable around here. It was hard enough switching the ovens from wood in the nineties." Somehow in their shifting around with the blankets she'd come closer to Rana. It should be awkward. She didn't know what this lady wanted besides a warm place. Why was she being so friendly? Rana's shoulder rested right next to hers, and her warmth seeped through the layers of cloth. The smell of warm tomatoes and cheese started drifting through the room as the fire chased some of the chill from the air. Everything about the situation was overwhelming and strange, and Marianne didn't know where to look.

"Thank you again for letting me impose," said Rana. "I hate to disturb your evening."

If someone had asked Marianne a week ago whether she was likely to welcome her neighbor into her home after simmering about the parking lot all autumn, she might have laughed in their face. But this woman wasn't anything like she'd expected. She'd built her up as some extension of Luke Leventi, some boogeyman through the wall, but instead—

She liked Rana. She was funny, smart, and she loved her kids, and she obviously knew how to cook. Maybe Marianne was getting soft, or maybe she was lonely, but something about Rana was very, very appealing to her.

She got up and shifted the pastries around and then stirred the marinara, which seemed to be heating nicely. "It's not much of a meal," she said regretfully. "But it's a nice little snack, at least."

"You don't have to feed me!" Rana laughed. "If I'd known this was what the service was like over here, I would have stopped by months ago!" She took the tray Marianne handed her. "Would you like me to slice? Where would I find a knife?"

Marianne handed her a serrated knife from the kitchen drawer, and Rana sliced half the loaf into neat one-inch cubes. Marianne was impressed: she didn't think she could have done that as quickly. She decided not to admit it, and instead took a piece of bread to dunk in the sauce. "So, tell me. What was Charleston like? I've never been south of Virginia."

"Hot," said Rana. "And I was not expecting the way people drive down there." She laughed. "You hear stories about Boston drivers, but they are so much better than in Charleston! Although the weather this time of year has much to recommend it, compared to Massachusetts."

Marianne leaned back into the couch, letting her shoulder rest against Rana's—for warmth, that's all—as Rana launched into a few examples of the dangerous Charleston streets. She listened, letting Rana's voice wash over her. It was soft and low and matched her perfectly, the slight accent not any impediment to understanding.

Marianne hadn't been attracted to anyone since she and Kevin had broken up—she'd thought about the occasional person idly, every once in a while, but the timing had never seemed right. But Rana's face in the candlelight—her broad cheekbones, her dark curls loose around her shoulders, her bright laugh—Marianne sat transfixed.

Rana finished the story, which had transitioned into an argument Joe Mitchell and Ray Bell had gotten into in her shop over the right of way rules at a certain intersection in town, and stretched out long fingers to pluck another piece of bread from the plate, dipping it in marinara before popping the piece into her mouth. Her eyes closed as she chewed, and Marianne let herself stare at the line of her throat and the curve of her jaw where glossy hair brushed olive skin. Her dark and sleek hair, mostly black with a scattering of white, hung in a heavy bun. Rana had a comfortably rounded shape with the same strong shoulders and legs Marianne herself had from decades in the kitchen. She didn't know what she'd imagined these past few months as neighbors: someone older, someone meaner, someone less beautiful? And Rana wasn't what she usually thought of as beautiful. If they'd passed on the street, Marianne might not have looked twice. But she glowed when she smiled, and she had a power in her shoulders and hips that made Marianne shiver.

It had been years since Marianne had kissed anyone, and it had been a lot longer since she'd kissed a woman. But sitting here in the near-dark, the warmth of the oven seeping up through the floor and into the upholstery of the couch and filling the air with the familiar scent of yeast and flour and home, she *wanted*. Oh, how she wanted. And she didn't even know what she wanted from Rana, besides closeness. Marianne had never been big on the physical side of relationships—it was something that had frustrated Kevin to no end. Sure, once in a blue moon someone struck her fancy: she found people attractive all the time, but with their clothes on. She wanted to look. She didn't usually want to touch.

Anna, her eldest, had a word for Marianne once she was old enough to have discussions with her mother on that kind of adult level after the questions raised by the divorce; she'd said that Marianne was probably somewhere on the asexual spectrum. Marianne had brushed the conversation aside, but it had stuck with her for years. She didn't quite know what to make of the idea. She had known she was bisexual her whole life, but this new dimension was a little scary to label. Having a way to describe how she felt might have made things easier once upon a time, back when she was dating and confused by not wanting all the things everyone else seemed to, but now? She didn't need to think about it that often.

But there was Rana, sitting beside her in the candlelight, smiling with sleepy, heavy-lidded eyes as she watched Marianne in the comfortable silence. And Marianne leaned in closer.

"I want to kiss you," said Rana, the straightforward words softened by the lilt of her accent. "Is that all right?"

Marianne's breath caught, and she nodded.

Rana stayed still for another moment, searching Marianne's face with dark brown eyes nearly black in the low light. Then she brought up her hand to brush back Marianne's hair, tucking it behind her shoulder, and kissed her.

Rana's lips were soft and dry, perfect against Marianne's own, and Marianne let her eyes close as she sank into Rana's embrace. They kissed for long enough that Marianne gasped for breath, and Rana's hands began to wander, sliding over the fabric of Marianne's shirt and slipping beneath the hem. Marianne loved the feeling of skin against her own, loved the warmth and intimacy of it, but when Rana's hand brushed the clasp of her bra she tensed and pulled back, shaking her head.

"I can go slow," whispered Rana. "If that's what you want."

"Can we keep things like this?" asked Marianne. "I don't think I want more than this."

It had been so long since she'd wanted anything more than a kiss from anyone. Honestly, she wasn't sure if she ever had, really. Sex with Kevin had been fine—fine enough to produce three children, but now that she was approaching sixty, she could admit sex hadn't ever been what she wanted for its own sake; only a way to be close to him. This fluttering in her stomach, this heat in her cheeks—that was terrifying, and if she didn't slow down, she didn't know what might happen.

Rana pulled away a bit, scrutinizing Marianne. "If you want to stop, you can tell me that," she said, the sultry tone fading.

"I don't!" Marianne caught her wrist and pulled her back in, feeling Rana's resistance melt away. "I just want to keep doing what we're doing. Is that okay? I don't want you to think I don't like you if I stop you later." If it wasn't—well, she'd gone years without wanting to kiss anyone. There was something between her and Rana—a spark, a tension—and part of her wanted to explore it, but another part was honestly terrified. She didn't know what she wanted. She had never really let herself think about what she wanted...and what she didn't.

Rana smiled, lips moist and dark, eyes filled with kindness and heat. "Certainly." She brushed a hand over Marianne's hair. "I like kissing you. If that's what you want, I'm happy to stay right here."

Chapter Three

Marianne woke slowly, noticing first that her right leg was asleep, and her left was freezing. Then she noticed the heavy weight all along her right side and the soft, sweet-smelling hair tickling her nostrils. As she tried to surreptitiously regain blood flow to her extremities, Rana stirred from where her head lay on Marianne's chest.

"Good morning." Rana's voice was huskier in the morning than it had been the night before. "Oh, I'm sorry. It seems I fell asleep on you."

"That's all right," said Marianne. She ran a gentle hand over Rana's hair, fingers sliding over the smooth strands.

"We don't have to get up," said Rana, eyes drifting closed again.

Marianne considered pulling herself free and getting up, but her leg had stopped tingling, and she'd found a more comfortable position on the old wide couch. She dozed back off.

The next thing she knew she was alone, a blanket tucked around her securely and sunlight streaming in the window. The fireplace was dark and cold; the last embers long since burned out.

"Rana?" she called quietly. No reply.

Marianne sat up and looked around, her pleasant sleepiness fading into the slightest frisson of anxiety. Did Rana leave? Had she done something wrong? She shook her head to clear it a little, pushing down the rising, tingling thread of panic winding its way through her stomach. Rana was an adult, and even if she had left, she had probably done so for a good reason.

The stairs creaked, and Rana appeared in the doorway holding a tray. "Hi," she said, cheeks pink and pants damp from the knee down. "I made breakfast. And a little bit of a mess on the floor by the door. Sorry. I couldn't find a mop."

"That's all right. Zeke keeps it in the customer bathroom, so it's not easy to find." She paused. "And besides, you're a guest. You shouldn't be cleaning." Marianne sat up, wincing at the tightness in her neck from a night on the couch.

Rana ignored the comment on doing the dishes. "Who is Zeke? One of your employees?"

Marianne laughed. "My only employee. He's been with me a few years, but he's Joe's great-grandson."

"Oh, Joe talks about him all the time!" Rana smiled, set the tray on the table, and sat beside Marianne. "The famous Ezekiel. I'll have to stop by and meet him some day. I didn't realize he worked for you. But first—" She gestured at the plate. "I hope you aren't a vegetarian," she said. "Just in case, I made one of the eggs without meat."

The eggs glistened, crisp fried edges and barely wobbling yolks, atop a pile of thin-sliced cured beef. Marianne's mouth watered at the savory smell. "You went all the way around the building?" she asked, realizing there was nothing like that in her kitchen.

Rana smiled a little awkwardly. "Just to get the meat from my shop," she said. "I cooked in your restaurant since the gas is still working. I hope that's all right. It was much warmer than mine, and brighter."

"I forgot how dim that room can get. We always meant to put in more windows but never got around to it. And if you're making food this good for me," said Marianne, picking up a fork, "you can use my kitchen any time."

"Is that a promise?" Rana sat beside Marianne, her knee brushing Marianne's. She wore the same clothes as the night before, close-fitting black-and-white patterned pants with a loose tunic that skimmed her curves. The silk of her blouse was slightly creased, and her hair mussed, but she looked even more beautiful than she'd been the night before.

There was something intimate about Rana using her kitchen. Marianne didn't know much about this woman besides that she could cook and had won over Joe and Ray, at least. Her hands on Marianne's tools though—her spatulas and pans and spoons? The thought made something warm curl in her chest. Below that feeling, Marianne's stomach growled.

"Eat," said Rana. "I made it for you." She picked up the second fork. "Of course, I also have to try them to make sure they taste right."

The eggs were, in fact, as delicious as they smelled. Garlicky and savory and peppery, the meat was the perfect complement, all cumin and fenugreek and paprika with the slightest hint of salty sourness. The thin slices were fried tender, chewy, and crisp at the same time. "If all your food tastes like this, it's no wonder your shop is so popular," said Marianne, swallowing. "Oh my god, Rana. This is so good!"

"I can't take credit for the basturma—the meat," she said. "A friend of mine makes it and sells it to me. But you should come try the hawawshi some time. If you like this, you'll love my pies. Since I assume you like things wrapped in bread?" The laugh lines around her eyes deepened, and in the morning sunlight Marianne noticed the faintest streaks of silver in her thick, dark hair.

"I wouldn't run a bakery if I didn't," Marianne replied. "That's a meat pie?"

"It's my best seller," said Rana. "A recipe from my grandmother. Come over when we get our power back and I'll make you one fresh, on the house." She smiled. "But you must be busy too. You're a town institution, I'm told. All that history!"

Marianne ate the last slice of meat and leaned back into the couch, content. "We've been here long enough to count, I guess." She waved at the walls around them. "I grew up here, you know. In this apartment."

"Right here?"

"This was our room, all the kids." Marianne looked at the mantle, where her childhood bunny and her cousin Johnny's wooden locomotive sat, a little worse for wear. "I hated it in the summer. You could never get the air cool enough since the heat came up through the floor."

Rana smiled. "You've lived here all your life?"

"Oh, goodness, no. My husband and I—ex-husband, now—had a house a few miles away. We sold it when we ended our marriage."

"I didn't know you used to be married," said Rana. "Is he still nearby?"

Marianne grinned suddenly, remembering Kevin's griping the previous day. "You kicked him out of your shop last week."

Rana frowned. "I don't remember kicking anyone out. I feel like I would remember that."

"Tall, gray hair, Kennedy smile?"

Rana considered it for a moment and then brightened. "Oh! He was whining about parking on the street. You were married to him?"

"That's the one."

"Well, he is attractive if you like men like that."

"I don't know that I do," said Marianne thoughtfully. "I think I knew *he* thought he was good-looking, and so I didn't bother checking for myself."

"Oh, I am sure he would love to hear you describe your marriage that way," said Rana. "He doesn't seem the type to appreciate a comment that insightful."

"He also wouldn't enjoy knowing you didn't remember him." Marianne tucked her feet under herself, tugging the blanket around her shoulders.

"Most men want to be remembered." Rana's face turned thoughtful. "My husband was a quiet man. He let me do all the talking. But he wanted to be remembered."

"He..." Marianne trailed off, not wanting to assume.

"He died, yes. A year before we came to the United States. He's been gone nearly twenty years now."

"You miss him."

Rana nodded. "I do. But it's been long enough that I can remember him and enjoy the reminder instead of just feeling the pain." She laughed suddenly. "Look at me, rambling about my husband when I've woken up with a beautiful woman. He'd call me a fool."

Her face warm, Marianne reached out and rested her hand over Rana's. "You're not a fool. I'm a good judge of that."

Outside the window, something heavy thudded to the ground. Marianne pulled herself away from Rana reluctantly and peered down at the street. "The snow's starting to melt off the roof," she said. "Maybe it'll fall off the powerlines, too, and we'll get electricity back."

"I hope so," said Rana, standing up and stretching. "Thank you for letting me stay with you," she said, turning to smile at Marianne. "I had a really lovely time last night. And this morning."

"Will I see you again?" The words spilled from Marianne, and she laughed a little. "I mean, not only as neighbors."

"I would like that." Rana leaned over and kissed Marianne's cheek with warm, dry lips. "Maybe I'll come over for some of that pie my customers keep telling me is so wonderful."

"And I'll be by for a meat pie one of these days." She smiled. "I know how busy you must be."

"I've been doing relatively well, yes, although not as well as you seem to be."

"Why do you say that?" Marianne gathered the plate and forks and stacked them together to take back to the kitchen.

"Well, I know the parking lot is always crowded."

"Most of my customers walk," said Marianne. "We never had a problem with the old neighbors."

"Well, my customers always say they'd come more often if they could park."

"They must not be telling you the truth then," said Marianne. "Because they're certainly parking in the lot like you are."

"Are you calling my customers liars?" Rana's eyes glittered, the flirty smile gone from her face. "I hope you are because otherwise you're calling me one."

"Nobody had a problem parking in that lot before the Grill moved in; that's all," said Marianne. "If you told them to move their cars when they finished eating—"

"Do you think they're parking all day?" Rana put her hands on her hips. "Why would they do that?"

"I don't know! Maybe they park there and go shopping in town!"

"Maybe your customers are the ones doing that!"

Marianne shook her head. "My customers know how to be polite," she snapped. "They don't take up space that's meant for other people."

"Are you saying I'm not allowed to use the parking lot? Because I don't see a 'Bakery Parking Only' sign anywhere, Ms. Windmere." She shook her head. "But I'm a tenant, not a city institution. I'm not from around here, not like you. I've only been in town six months, not sixty years. What do I know." She gathered her coat from the chair it had been drying on. "I think it's time for me to leave. I know where I'm not wanted."

Marianne crossed her arms, stomach turning sour, and didn't reply, just watching as Rana gathered her things and disappeared out the door. How had the wonderful morning gone so wrong?

The scent of garlic, paprika, and cumin lingered in the air from the eggs and the turnovers the night before. Marianne picked up the dishes and slowly walked them down to the kitchen.

They were the only businesses on the block. All the residents had driveways. Farther down Main Street, toward the center of town, street parking was plentiful. And the train station had its own giant lot. Why would Rana be so sure it wasn't her customers?

Guilt sat in Marianne's chest like stubborn heartburn, nagging her throat. She was used to that feeling–an automatic reaction to arguments ingrained in her by years of society pushing the notion that ladies stayed calm and let things go. But that wasn't all.

She hadn't liked someone like that in a long time, and she'd somehow chosen precisely the wrong person to feel one of her unexpected and rare moments of attraction to. And now that person was gone, back to her side of the building, and Marianne probably wouldn't see her again. She groaned and got out the shovel to clear the front walkway.

Chapter Four

Marianne had been up and down the stairs all day and hadn't heard a peep from the Cairo Grill side of the wall. Despite everything, she hoped Rana had gotten home safely instead of shivering in her still-powerless bakery. Their building was close enough to the main road that she shouldn't have too much unplowed territory to get through, and the sun was already melting parts of the snow over the asphalt. According to the electric company's website, the bakery would be getting power back within a few hours. If it did, she could start serving coffee. And she could start muffins now, at least, in the old gas oven. People would appreciate that in weather like this.

Marianne glanced out the window, catching the sun starting to peek out through the clouds on the pristine sheets of snow past the train tracks. Out front, Ray was already out plowing, cutting neat lines through the parking lot on his way back out to the roads. She waved down when she saw him glance up, and he grinned and waved back. On the tracks, a snowblower rolled by and shot gray piles of slush to either side of the rails.

She knew she should get up and open the bakery doors, knew that she'd have customers soon enough who depended on her bakery in weather like this, but it wasn't appealing today. She pulled her old robe tighter around her shoulders, shivering. The heat from the stove below had finally dissipated, leaving her apartment chilly and quiet as a tomb. At least if she got the old stove going, it would warm up the building. It would even help shake the worst of the chill from where Rana had sat beside her last night.

No, Marianne wasn't going to think about Rana. She wasn't. She barely knew the woman. She'd had some kind of bizarre lapse, kissing her nemesis, and now she was paying for her behavior with all of these thoughts that didn't do her any good.

She shed her robe and got dressed, going for warmth over fashion, and headed down the steps into the bakery. It looked forlorn in the morning light, its counters crumb covered and the trash full. She sighed, rolled up her sleeves, switched on the gas, and got to work. The old monster sputtered and caught when she touched the match to the pilot. She sent a silent thank-you to her grandfather for picking an oven that would last eighty years, and to her father for retrofitting it to 1980s safety standards so none of them would blow the bakery up trying to use it.

Tori Shapiro, the town's veteran librarian, knocked on the door a few minutes past nine. Marianne unlocked it, letting her in.

"Hey, honey," said Tori, kissing Marianne's cheek. "I don't mean to be pushy, but if I don't get some coffee before work, I'm going to murder someone. I love my children, but they're monsters on a snowy day."

Marianne laughed and pulled out the French press and ground coffee, sticking a kettle on the gas stove to boil. "All this snow and you have to work?"

Tori shook her head. "You would think being the boss would mean I could avoid coming in on days like this one. But no. No power, and all this snow means there might be problems. So, Lila's home with the kids while I'm stuck at the office watching for leaks."

"Remember when snow days were fun?" Marianne poured the hot water over the grounds, letting them steep. "I wonder if kids still sled over at the high school."

"Not since they built that new development out there," said Tori. "They'd land right in the swimming pool if they tried sledding where we used to." She leaned her elbows on the counter, tucking her long auburn hair back behind her ear. "Remember when Kevin ran right into the mayor's car?"

Marianne laughed as she plunged the press down. "He never confessed. I think the mayor knew it was him, but he could never prove it. Kevin used to avoid him every winter, just in case his guilt would show somehow, or he'd blurt a confession out." She handed Tori a paper cup that steamed with hot coffee. "Honey in there, right?" She pulled out a jar. "I'll let you do the honors."

Tori brought the cup up to her nose, eyes fluttering shut as she breathed in. Taking the honey, she grinned at Marianne. "At least they can't get up to the kind of trouble we did back then, now that that old shed is gone." She patted Marianne's hand. "Ah, our wild youths. Thank goodness that's over." She straightened. "Thanks for the coffee, M. You're a lifesaver. I'll let folks know you're open." She dug out her wallet and handed Marianne a five. "Keep the change. This was worth it."

"Just make sure they know the internet's out, so I can't take cards, okay?"

"I'll tell people you're cash only." Tori took a long sip of the coffee before tugging her coat collar up closer around her neck and turning toward the door. "Wish me luck in the cold, dark library."

*

Zeke shuffled in around ten, shaking snow from his boots and shivering as he slung his backpack into the chair in her office and hung his coat on a peg to drip dry. "Warming up out there," he observed, rubbing his hands together. "What's up, boss? Power's not back yet?"

Marianne shook her head. "They say it'll be back soon, but who knows? Yours is out too?"

He nodded. "I set Granddad up with the woodstove, and Ms. Shapiro's gonna check on him too. Uh, Lila, not Tori. Tori's wife." He snorted. "That's one reason not to change your name."

"Doris will probably stop in on him too," said Marianne. "I'll mention it when she comes by. Or I'll let you mention it." She glanced out the window. The sun shone bright against the snow. "Don't know if we'll get many customers today, so if you want to leave early, let me know."

He shrugged. "I need the money more than the time." He washed his hands and dried them on a paper towel, tossing the paper in a graceful arc into the trash can across the room.

Marianne turned, putting her hands on her hips. "What did I say about throwing flammables near the stove?"

Zeke scratched the back of his neck. "Not to?"

"That's right."

"It was a good shot though," he pointed out.

Marianne shook her head. "Good shot or not, I'm not burning this place down so you can make the basketball team."

He cocked his head. "You look weird, boss."

This time she did laugh. "That's exactly what every woman wants to hear, Zeke."

"You okay?" The question was unexpectedly soft, and Marianne suddenly felt herself blinking back the beginnings of tears. It had been a strange, fraught morning after a weird, wonderful night.

"I'm all right, Zeke." She cleared her throat and patted him on the shoulder as she pulled down a new tub of shredded cheddar from the fridge. "Let's get some work done, okay? I'll start cooking if you start shoveling."

Just as Marianne pulled the first tray of muffins from the oven, the bell on the door jingled. She heard the cash register ding as she came around the corner to find Jesse Laurence chatting with Zeke as he poured sugar into his coffee.

Jesse was someone who'd always been around, another town fixture like herself who'd been born in Swanley and would die there. His family and hers had never really gotten along, but the last few years she'd come to appreciate his dry humor and his devil-may-care attitude toward the rest of the world. When they'd been in school together, he'd had a chip on his shoulder the size of Texas. He'd mellowed since meeting his partner in his late thirties, growing up more in the two decades since than she ever expected him to.

"Jesse! How's Jo?" she asked, brushing her hands off on her apron. "Haven't seen them around lately."

Jesse grinned. "Hey there, Ms. Marianne! We're good. They're outta town. Enjoying the sun down in

Arizona with their sister. Some kind of bonding something, I don't know, but they're glad to be missing the snow." He held up the coffee Zeke handed him. "Hey, thanks for being open. I needed this."

"You know I'm always here." She waved as he pulled his jacket closer in around himself. Marianne watched him go, envying the ease with which he moved through the town and its politics despite having dreams of moving away when he was younger. She wished she'd been able to let go of hers so easily. She loved Swanley, but being here in her grandfather's apron in her family's hundred-and-fifty-year-old business was not the life of travel and excitement outside small-town Massachusetts she'd hoped for at twenty.

She pushed back through the doors and pulled another pair of muffin trays out, cheddar-chive and cranberry, and set them on racks to cool. There was something oddly satisfying about cooking in the old green monster of a stove though. Its heavy-hinged doors swung smoothly after a little grease, and the blasting heat gave the muffins a crisp top that the newer electric stoves couldn't quite achieve. She felt like her grandfather and father were cooking beside her when she used it, and the feeling was comforting rather than stifling. She popped out a cheddar muffin, juggling it from hand to hand, and bit into its steaming top. There was nothing in the world like a hot baked good.

*

A week later, the snow still hung around the parking lot and sidewalks, gray with mud and dirt and freezing solid every night to melt to progressively larger puddles every afternoon. Marianne had shoveled the front as best she could, but the ice kept reappearing. She lived in terror of being sued when some commuter inevitably slipped.

On the other side of the wall, she heard movement. It sounded like someone digging through metal pans. She tried to block out the sound. She didn't need to remember Rana's hands against her own, or the softness of her skin. She needed to forget anything had ever happened. The few glances of Rana she'd caught through the window of the Cairo Grill had left her frazzled, and she didn't need that.

She hurried on up the stairs, past the sounds, back to her apartment. That new cookbook from Jacob might be in her bedroom, and she'd need it if she was going to try the cherry tart recipe. Zeke would have to handle the customers for the moment—she needed a little break and a little peace.

Someone honked in the distance, and Marianne automatically looked out the window. Down below her, pulling into a spot right beside the entrance to the bakery, was a big black BMW that Marianne recognized as a frequent parker in the lot. She knew that car. It always parked right outside the door to Rana's shop for hours at a time, hogging one of the few precious spots big enough for an SUV. She *hated* that car.

Marianne watched closely as the door to the SUV popped open, and a bald, stocky white man in a suit stepped out, glancing at his watch and pulling a briefcase from the seat beside him. He closed the door, locked the car with a quick tap of the button, and headed—

Across the street. He barely paused in the crosswalk, hurrying to stand under the streetlight half a block down Main Street. And below, another car pulled in—this one a green hatchback—and two women in blouses and blazers followed suit. The first man shook the hand of each woman, clapping one on the shoulder as the other pulled out her phone. The woman in the red skirt—she looked familiar. Marianne squinted down. Was that Callie Fern? What in the world was the Chief of Police's daughter doing parking in her lot? She certainly wasn't stopping by the bakery or by the Cairo Grill—if Marianne remembered correctly from Anna's school days, the girl was vegan and didn't eat gluten. Not a lot she could eat at either place, though Marianne was trying to improve her allergen-friendly menu.

As another two cars came around the corner and pulled into the driveway to the lot, Marianne's stomach filled with a peculiar sinking feeling. She might have made an assumption that was not entirely correct. In fact, she might have been making assumptions for months. *Could I really have been wrong about this the whole time?*

And then a vehicle pulled up, a white passenger van that glittered against the dirty snow, and the people whose cars were clogging her lot climbed in.

Marianne raced down the steps, pulling her jacket on and shoving her feet into boots as she jumped in her car and started it up. As she pulled out of the parking lot, she could see the back of the van as it turned down Oak Street.

"I hope the cops are sleeping in," she muttered as she gunned the engine down Main Street to make the light.

There was that van again, taking a left onto Milton Avenue. She followed it, merging a few cars back as it pulled onto the highway on-ramp. "Where are you going?" she asked aloud, trailing behind and feeling like some kind of TV private eye.

The mystery van pulled off an exit later and pulled into the massive new complex that had gone up in

Wilshire a few months previous, stopping in front of the CoffeeGuru sign. She knew the business. They had some kind of app for avoiding lines at coffee shops, or something like that. They'd been buying up land in Wilshire and, apparently, not converting any of it into parking. As she watched, another two vans pulled up, depositing more business-casual people in front of the door.

Marianne pulled into a spot across from the building and watched the hip young people file in, taking a few quick photos on her phone. As the door shut behind Callie, she pulled up the emergency brake and slowly lowered her face until her forehead rested on the steering wheel. She hated being wrong, and she hated apologizing for it. She started the car back up and drove back to the bakery, slowly this time. This was some kind of work shuttle then from the center of town to the new building for the company. So she'd been blaming Rana these past few months for nothing. Marianne tried to press down the anxiety acid in her stomach.

The lights were still out in Rana's front window, and Marianne stopped at the door, unsure how to proceed. Finally, she knocked on the locked glass door, shivering a little in the chilly air. "Rana?" she called through the door. "Are you there? Can I talk to you?" Rana's car had been in its usual spot in the lot—the lot which was now completely filled, despite only one store in the building being open and that one nearly empty—and Marianne had taken a moment to marvel at how the sight of that big silver hatchback used to fill her with simmering rage. Now it was a conflicted sight, evoking guilt, butterflies in her stomach, and a fondness that went deeper than she'd expected after knowing each other just one day. She knocked again and then shook her head. She was about to turn away and trudge back around the building when the light flicked on and the door swung open. Rana peered out, squinting in the sun. "Yes?" she said and then stiffened. "Oh. Ms. Windmere."

"I'm sorry." The words came out in a rush. "It's not your customers. You were right."

"Hm." Rana crossed her arms and leaned against the doorframe. "So, your customers weren't as blameless as you thought."

"No!" Marianne shook her head, trying not to get annoyed. "No, see, that's the thing. It's not my customers either."

As if on cue, a white van drove by.

Marianne pointed at the vehicle as it slowed and stopped. "It's them."

Rana's eyes widened. "What?"

"It's that building off the highway in Wilshire. You know the one, with the obnoxious windows that make seeing anything impossible when you drive by at sunset?"

"Oh, I know it."

Marianne pulled out her phone, holding it out to show Rana the picture she'd taken of the van in front of the office building. "They're doing some sort of shuttle service and using us as their free lot."

Rana leaned in to look, her shoulder pressing into Marianne's.

"Those cheats!" Rana huffed. "That is *rude*." She smiled slightly, flicking her eyes to Marianne's. "You look like a woman with a plan to fix this."

"You aren't angry?"

Rana pulled away, leaving Marianne cold. She glanced down the street, frustration and tiredness flickering over her face. "Marianne—" She shook her head. "I'm hurt that you assumed it was me. I'm annoyed you never bothered to visit my shop to ask. And I'm frustrated it's taken us this long to figure out what the problem is. But angry? No. Not at you. I'm mostly tired." She met Marianne's eyes, a challenge in her gaze. "And I have a feeling you're going to do something about this, aren't you?"

"I'm going to try." Marianne smiled tentatively. "I'm not sure how to fix this. I have some ideas of where to start; that's all."

"Well then. How can I help?"

Marianne blinked. "You want to help?"

Rana shrugged. "It's my parking lot too. Believe me my customers aren't any happier about the situation. I always believed it was your customers. If I can send these commuters on their way, it's good for everyone."

"Well, what we need is a sign; I think." said Marianne. Warmth had built in her stomach, relief mixing with anticipation. "Something like the one at the pharmacy. You know, Customer Parking Only, a note like that."

"Is that something we can buy? I suppose not, if we want it enforced." Rana leaned forward, interested. "Who do we ask?"

Marianne laughed. "I'm not sure, but we can figure it out. Give me a day."

"I'll make us dinner tomorrow," said Rana, a dimple appearing in her brown cheek as she smiled. "Meat pies and salad. And you can give me the update then."

Marianne smiled back, warm and delighted.

Chapter Five

Marianne Windmere was a woman on a mission.

The first thing she needed to do was call city hall. She knew a few older members of the city council from back when Kevin was a councilor, back when they were married, but she hadn't spoken to them in so long she thought it might be rude to ask for a favor out of the blue.

So, she called the main number instead, following the menus to the parking clerk, who very politely informed her that his office only handled parking tickets, not parking rules. He suggested she call the police if people were parking illegally in her lot. That seemed extreme. Marianne tried not to get the police involved in anything she didn't have to. Personally, the few she knew seemed like all-right guys, but power did strange things to people. Besides, she wasn't sure if any crimes were being committed. It wasn't as if the lot was marked private or anything. And a small part of her, the part that watched too much news late at night, wondered about the wisdom of bringing the police into a dispute that involved a recent Middle Eastern immigrant. It just gave her a bad feeling.

Next, she tried Ray, who plowed the parking lot in the winter. He sounded apologetic. "I'm not sure who'd be in charge of that, hon," he said. "Do you own the lot, or is it town property?"

Marianne paused. Did she own it? She'd never thought about it. The store and the front walk, that was hers. But the lot? "If it isn't town property, would you still have to plow it?"

Ray laughed. "I've been plowing your lot every storm for the last thirty years like I do every other lot in the town center. I got no idea which ones I'm technically supposed to do anymore." Marianne heard a truck starting up in the background. "But that's probably where you've got to start. Maybe the Assessor?"

She should have thought of that. If anyone would know what she owned, it'd be the people in charge of taxing her on it. She flipped through the town report until she found a number for them and dialed it. The woman who picked up didn't seem thrilled to be getting a call.

"Hi, this is Marianne Windmere," said Marianne. "I'm trying to find some information."

"What kind of information?"

"I want to know who owns my parking lot."

"What's the address?"

"121A Main Street in Swanley."

Silence on the line.

"Hello?"

"Windmere Bakery?" The woman sounded a little annoyed. "Don't you have your deed?"

"My deed? Um..." Marianne looked around the office. The taxes from the last fifteen years and all her purchase orders and her reports were filed in the big metal filing cabinets by the door, but she knew there wasn't anything that predated her running the business in there. Upstairs in her apartment's unheated storeroom sat her father's old wooden filing cabinet, stuffed to the brim with barely organized piles and folders of mingled personal and business records. She'd been meaning to clean the office out for years, to send some of the more interesting pages and photos to Anna, the only one of her kids with any interest in the family history. She figured that would be a good place to start.

Papers rustled on the other end of the phone, interspersed with clacking. "The last survey I have on the property is from—huh."

"What?" Marianne didn't like the sound of that *huh*.

"The last survey I'm seeing for 121 Main Street is 1964," said the woman. A note of surprise colored her voice. "If we haven't done a survey since, we'll need your deed to initiate a new one."

"What if I can't find it?"

"If you can't find it, you can't prove ownership, and for a property that's been unsold this long, you may have a problem."

"My family has run this business for over a century in the same exact spot!" Marianne protested. "And my father sold part of the property in 1968. Surely there are records of that, at least, somewhere at city hall?"

"Sorry, we don't do that sort of research here," she said. "You'd need to file an application for a record search." She didn't sound sorry. Not for the first time, Marianne wished Swanley was one of those hip modern suburbs with online websites and stuff. Not that she'd know how to use them if they did. But maybe her son Jacob could have helped.

"I thought you had some kind of records database or something?"

The woman huffed, a little more sympathetic, perhaps, now that she knew Marianne wasn't going to be so easily put off. "Ma'am, when something is bought or sold, we have a record of it. If the sale happened before the 1980s, it's not in the database. We haven't digitized so far back, and many of the records were lost in the flood in '92, or the fire in '76. So no, there's no information we can find here."

"What about tax records? Don't you know how much to charge me for?"

"We have the value of your property. We don't have specific property boundary information." In the background, Marianne heard another phone ringing. "If you can bring us a deed, we can give you more information."

Marianne sensed she wasn't going to get any better answer. "Well, I guess I'll look around," she said, doubtfully.

"You have a nice day." She hung up with a click.

"You too," said Marianne into the empty receiver. She glanced up at the clock and grimaced. She'd spent the whole afternoon, from closing time at four to nearly six thirty, on useless calls. Rana would be wondering where she was.

Her heart lightened a little at the thought, though she fought the hope down. It was better to keep things friendly between them. What was she doing, flirting with strangers at her age and having awkward morning afters? She'd never even done that in her twenties. One night of kissing, and she was acting like a teenager. Besides, she had to admit, at least to herself, that she could use a friend who hadn't known her when she and Kevin were married. Everyone else in town knew her as either Daniel's youngest daughter or Kevin's ex-wife. They each had their own opinions about why Marianne and Kevin's marriage hadn't worked. In a town of less than six thousand, most of whom had been born within ten miles of each other, nobody had any private business. Gossip didn't require a

forty-minute drive to the movie theater in Framingham—
it was free.

Her phone rang, the cheerful little ringtone Anna had
programmed for herself, and Marianne smiled as she
answered. "Hi, sweetie."

"Hey, Mom." Anna sounded a little out of breath like
she'd been hurrying down a flight of stairs or something.
Marianne repressed her maternal instinct to ask her if she
had her inhaler and to remind her to sit down and rest if
she needed it. "You busy?"

"Never too busy for my girl. Everything all right?"

"Oh, yeah. I wanted to see how you were doing. Dad
said you were having some trouble with the property."

"He did, did he?"

"And he figured that if you wouldn't let him help, you
might want to talk to me about it."

"Why's that?"

Anna sighed. "Come on, Mom. He wants to be useful.
You know that. He wants to help."

Marianne gathered the papers from the day's work
and filed them and then shrugged on her jacket. She was
only walking a few dozen feet around the building, but the
weather promised a cold night ahead. "I know, sweetie.
But I've got it handled."

"Are you sure? I've designed some pretty neat
parking structures, you know."

Marianne smiled. "My little I. M. Pei."

"I'd prefer to go with Frank Lloyd Wright, at least. I
try not to use much concrete. Brutalism's a little out of
vogue, Mom."

"You're better than either of them." Marianne opened
the front door and shivered, tucking her jacket closer
around her.

"Are you on your way somewhere? I hear wind."

"Dinner with a friend," said Marianne. "But I can talk as long as you like."

"Oh, no. I won't keep you! But let me know if I can help."

"I will. Love you, sweetie."

"Love you, too, Mom, and I'm glad you're getting out and about. It's not good for you to stay in the bakery all the time."

"You sound like *my* mother now. Good night."

There was a smile in Anna's voice. "Night."

Marianne hung the phone up and stuffed it in her pocket, tucking the bag of pastries under her arm a little tighter as she fought the wind and slush to the front door of Rana's restaurant. Now that she thought about it a little more, it *was* odd she'd never been in here, not since Rana had taken over from that really terrible sub shop that had been there previously. And before that, the pasta bar, then the chopped salads, the noodle place, the stationery store, the fried chicken—she hadn't realized quite how often the space had turned over, all the jokes about its curse aside. But Rana's front windows were warm and welcoming, a lone customer sitting at the bar—she had a bar, brilliant— and Rana behind the counter, wiping down her work surfaces with a damp cloth.

Marianne pushed open the door and stepped inside, letting the warmth of the restaurant shake the chill from her fingers. For a moment, her stomach clenched with anxiety. She didn't know this woman much at all. Had Rana really forgiven her their argument so easily?

Rana looked up and smiled. "Took you long enough," she said. "Everything all right?"

The customer turned around. "Marianne!" Ray had a giant plate of meat in front of him, garnished with a few cucumbers. Marianne winced internally for his stents. His vegetarian nurse of a wife wouldn't be thrilled he was downing a pound of lamb this late in the evening. He looked so guilty—the same face his German Shepherd made when she got caught in the compost again—that Marianne decided she wouldn't tell on him. She gave him a smile.

"Hey, Ray. Long day?"

He hesitated, watching her for a moment to see if she'd say anything and then shrugged. "Oh, just the usual. Wanted to come out and try Rana's shawarma though. I heard it was great."

"And?"

He grinned. "I'll be back even if I have to bribe you not to tell Kathy."

Marianne laughed. "Hey, none of my business what you tell your wife, Ray." She turned to Rana. "Hi."

Rana tucked her long hair behind an ear. "Hi."

Ray glanced from one to the other and pushed himself up with a groan. "Rana, could I grab a box for this? I'm gonna put it in my work fridge for lunch tomorrow. High time I got out of here, I think."

"You're welcome to stay," said Rana. "I'm closing for customers, but I'm open for friends."

"Thanks, but no. I really do have to go home." Ray stretched, wincing as he turned his back from side to side. Rana slid his leftovers into the aluminum container. "I appreciate the invitation though. And the food." He tucked the container in the bottom of his lunch bag and gave them both a wave as he left.

"So, what did you find out?" asked Rana, bringing out a pair of clean ceramic plates with a gorgeous red-and-blue geometric pattern and then a big platter with meats, grilled tomatoes, fried cauliflower, and what looked like falafel. Beside it, she placed a bowl of cucumbers, peppers, and tomatoes sprinkled with feta.

"Jeez, is there an army coming I don't know about?" Marianne surveyed the mounds of food in front of her. "Or do you have a secret life as a competitive eater?"

Rana shrugged, settling into the seat across from her in the booth. "I thought you might want to taste a variety of things, since you hadn't come by yet."

"Sorry about that," said Marianne. "I don't usually come to whatever restaurant is renting the space."

"Why not? I was sort of offended. It didn't seem very neighborly." Rana took the spoon and started loading the plates. Marianne reached to help but was stilled with a look. "Oh, the bread!" She reached back over the counter and found a basket of small round pitas. "Here." She held the basket out to Marianne, who took one and placed it on the very edge of her towering plate.

"It wasn't," said Marianne. She copied Rana, who layered meat and vegetables on her bread and then drizzled sauce over it all. "I wasn't exactly gracious. My family has been bitter about this place for a long time."

Rana looked up from her food, surprise flashing across her face. "Bitter? Why? The parking lot issue?"

"That's only been the last few months." Marianne took a bite as she considered how to answer. The spice and depth of flavor of the meat and sauce shocked her out of her train of thought, her eyes drifting closed as she savored. "Oh my god, Rana," she said when she finally swallowed. "This is incredible. How had I not been here before?"

Rana laughed a little. "Family bitterness, I'm told."

"I'll explain in a minute once I've tried this salad." Unsurprisingly, the salad was also delicious, light and tangy with vinegar and cumin.

"I would have saved you some hawawshi, but I sold out today," said Rana apologetically. "I'll bring some by later in the week if you'd like."

"Are those your meat pies? People have been talking about those nonstop." Marianne leaned back against the booth's vinyl. "You're singlehandedly increasing the spice tolerance of our little town, you know."

"My food isn't spicy!"

"For Swanley? It's nuclear. This town is a steak and potatoes kind of place usually. But I'd give up both for this meatball thing."

"Kofta," said Rana, cheek dimpling as she smiled. "And you keep dodging my question. What's wrong with my store?"

Marianne sighed. "It used to be ours. That's all."

"That makes sense," said Rana thoughtfully. "I had wondered why a bakery that had been in the town as long as yours has would have a little rental like this. At first I thought Mr. Leventi owned your bakery too—"

"I know you did, and don't even joke about that!" Marianne shuddered. "He'd love to get his hands on the bakery, and he never, ever will even if I have to live to be a hundred to outlast him."

"I found out he didn't very quickly!" said Rana. "Your friend Ray gave me hell when I mentioned my mistake. I promise."

"Good old Ray," Marianne said. "As well he should. Ray's no friend of the Leventi family either."

"I get the feeling not many people are."

"Enough are," said Marianne. "Just not the ones I prefer to spend time with. Otherwise, they wouldn't be as powerful as they are." She shook her head. "Powerful people always have friends. Doesn't matter who they are."

"That's true everywhere in the world I'm afraid. So, if the old grudge isn't about the lot, then what is it? And speaking of the lot, I'm still waiting for you to give me your update! What did you find out about the parking situation?" Rana set her now empty plate to one side and rested her elbows on the table, leaning forward over crossed arms.

"Unfortunately, not much. They won't tell me anything without proof I own the lot."

Rana frowned. "Isn't ownership of property public information?"

"Apparently real estate transactions are public information, but if those transactions happened before the current system was in place, it's not so easy. That seems to be true for a lot of places that were bought before the eighties. And because it's not just a sale, it's a splitting of a lot, I'm going to guess it's more complicated." Marianne spooned a little more of the salad onto her plate. "Rana, this is so good."

"I'm glad you like it." Rana's cheeks dimpled. "So, you're saying because you've owned it longer than forty years, they can't tell you for sure you own it? Even though you pay taxes on it?"

"I guess they can't tell me how much of the land I own. They know I own some of the lot and how much that part of the lot is worth. I guess they increase it by the amount of inflation every year, or something like that." She shrugged. "I'm not sure where to go from here. Even if I do have a deed, a bill of sale, or a receipt or something, I have no idea where my dad would have put it."

"I didn't have much luck either." Rana sighed. "I called CoffeeGuru's contact number. I thought they'd want to know they were alienating the locals."

"That's a great idea!"

"Maybe, but I didn't get anywhere. I explained the problem—I thought maybe they'd want to know where their customers were parking and perhaps they'd put up some sort of sign saying not to park in the town for the shuttle, but they said they can't make any statements about any parking spot they don't own. They were not very helpful. They said if I wanted to file a complaint, I'd have to talk to their legal department."

"And it's the same problem we have here. We can't prove we own it, so we can't complain."

"Are you sure you do?"

Marianne opened her mouth to answer and then closed it and considered the question. "I'm pretty sure." Two years ago, she'd had the thing paved, and the bill had been enormous. If it turned out she was doing someone else's work for them—well, she wouldn't be thrilled. "And my father wouldn't have sold it."

"Why did he sell any of it, anyway?"

"He didn't want to." Marianne straightened her napkin on the table with restless fingers. "At least, I don't think he did." She paused to gather her thoughts.

"If you don't want to tell me—"

"It's all right." Marianne surprised herself with her vehemence. "I mean—it's been so long since I thought about it, about that time. I was nine then. I didn't know what was going on. Just that my dad had been away for a long time and he came back much sadder. He fought in Vietnam and came home in 1968, and I hadn't seen him in more than a year. And then a few months later, he sold part of the bakery to Simon Leventi."

"That's Luke's dad?"

"Exactly. They've been big landlords in town my whole life." She shook her head. "He and my dad were friends, though I can't imagine how now. Maybe he was different when they were young. And I guess Simon seemed like a nice enough guy when I was a kid. But when my dad got sick, he paid Simon to run the place. He didn't get drafted, or he got out of it somehow, so he wasn't a mess like the rest of the guys his age. And I guess he made a lot of money while my dad was away because when dad got back and needed money, Simon offered to buy the other storefront and keep running our half until I was old enough to take over. I came back to take the bakery back in '92, but he kept your part."

"So, that's why he owns my suite but not yours." Rana looked thoughtful. "But you don't know if your father sold the parking lot as well."

"Exactly. And now I can't even find proof my dad owned the lot in the first place."

"Maybe he didn't."

"He had it paved when I was thirteen or so," said Marianne. "And I've paved it twice more. And painted its lines." She shook her head. "If I don't own it, that's a lot of money the city should be paying me back."

"Or my landlord."

"Exactly."

Rana picked up the dishes and stacked them neatly on a tray. Marianne rose automatically to help, gathering napkins and glasses and bringing them around the counter behind Rana. Rana's red-checked apron tied neatly around her waist, a nice touch of homey, classic-diner fashion Marianne found adorable.

She found everything about Rana adorable, actually, and not for the first time, she wished she'd behaved better after their night together. That snowy evening lay misty in her mind, and sometimes she wondered if she'd dreamed kissing that perfect mouth and holding those long, elegant hands. Rana was so different from Kevin, but no less stubborn and competent. If Marianne's few crushes had anything in common, it was competence. She loved a person who knew what they were doing.

She followed Rana to the sink and grabbed a fresh towel from a cabinet above the drying rack. "Would you like me to dry?"

Rana glanced up, seemingly startled to have company in the kitchen. "Oh, you don't have to."

"I'd like to," said Marianne. "I ate, you cooked, and the least I can do is help clean up."

Rana looked unconvinced. "How about you keep me company instead? I like things done the way I do them." She smiled. "But I'd love to have someone to talk to."

Marianne was happy to do that much.

Chapter Six

Zeke clomped in through the front door the next morning, letting in a blast of cold air as he shoved the door closed and shook snow off his boots onto the mat in the entryway. "It's freezing out there!" he called to Marianne, who'd poked her head through the kitchen door when she'd heard the bell over the entrance jingle. "Just me, no customers." He shivered. "They're saying we're in for another week of this damn arctic weather. So business might stay slow."

"I wouldn't be out in this weather either," said Marianne. "We had a little rush earlier when the sun came out. Sold out of hot cocoa and cider."

Zeke groaned. "Really?"

"Not quite." Marianne smiled. "I saved you a cider, don't worry."

He gave her a thumbs-up as he peeled himself out of his coat and slung it over a chair. In the warmth of the bakery, the snow on his collar and sleeves immediately started melting into a puddle on the floor. "I'll clean that up," he reassured her. "Hey, the parking lot is looking a lot less full today."

Marianne gave him a look. "You know the train's not running today, right? Because of the storm?"

He winced. "Ah. Sorry. I thought maybe the city got off their asses and did something."

"Well, we haven't made much progress yet, but Ray came by and plowed anyway. I hope they won't make him stop now that we've started asking questions."

"Ray loves you." Zeke started stacking baking trays to bring to the dishwasher. "He'd plow you out even if they told him not to." He stopped for a moment at Marianne's muffled snort and then rolled his eyes, not amused. "That didn't come out right."

"Anyway." Marianne suppressed a laugh. She had *some* dignity to maintain, after all. "I'm thinking of making one myself. A sign, I mean."

"Can you do that?"

"It's my building. If I hang something on my wall, it's my business." She sighed. "I have to figure out how to make a sign now."

"I can help!" Zeke abandoned his efforts to fit the baking sheets in the dishwasher, grabbing his computer from his backpack instead. "We have to get a nice laminated piece of board, is that all?"

"That would survive the winter, right? It wouldn't melt in the first snow?"

"It should." Zeke pulled up an art program and started typing.

"No commuter parking," read Marianne. "Hey, that looks good!"

Zeke smiled. "I took a design class last year," he explained. "I've been practicing on band logos for my friends' groups, but this is cooler, mostly because I'm a giant nerd." He pulled up a browser window and searched for parking signs, scanning them quickly and formatting his the same way. "Okay, I can print this out at school for you."

"What would I do without you?" asked Marianne as the door jingled again, heralding the arrival of three actual customers.

Grinning, Zeke clapped her on the shoulder on his way to the register to meet the customers. "You're not going to find out any time soon."

She watched him sell a bag of assorted pastries and a baguette to the customers, a tall ginger man she'd seen around a few times in the last week and two younger white brunettes, and then he poured the coffees they'd ordered and passed them over the counter.

"Really, Zeke, I'm going to be in trouble when you move away."

"Who says I'm going to move away?" asked Zeke. "I'm going to be just like Joe, bothering your grandkids' customers someday."

"I hope I can get somebody to take over the place before my nonexistent grandkids," said Marianne. "I'd better not be behind this counter when I'm ninety. If I am, you better take me out back like *Old Yeller*."

"One of your kids'll step up eventually." Zeke gestured up at the thick oak beams crossing the ceiling, weathered from a century and a half of steam and history. "They can't let this place disappear. Don't worry, I'll bribe them or threaten them or something. I like this job too much."

Marianne was about to reply when the bell over the door rang. Marianne's calm evaporated when she caught sight of who was shaking snow from his coat in her entryway.

Luke Leventi didn't spend much time in town these days. He was campaigning for the soon-to-be open House of Representatives seat and spent most of his time in the surrounding towns where he wasn't quite so well known.

"Marianne," he said, the joviality almost believable. "How's business?"

"Lucas," she replied, trying to keep the smile on her face as natural as it had been with Zeke. "What can I do for you?"

"Hmm." He leaned in, ignoring the customers in the corner eyeing him curiously. The race had been hard-fought so far, the polls showing Leventi and Hechevarria neck and neck for the lead. People outside of Massachusetts had started paying attention, and locally, the election was the biggest news since Shari Ng's llamas had gotten loose and stopped traffic on I-695.

Marianne fought the eye roll that tried to escape at the fuss the girls were making. He cut a striking figure in his suit and wingtips, and he *had* been making the rounds on the local news circuit lately, but that didn't mean they had to be so obvious about it.

"An apple Danish, I think," said Leventi. "Do you still use all local apples?"

"For a few more weeks anyway," said Marianne. "Until I run out of the ones from Collins Farm. I like to keep things in the county." She pulled one out and put it in a bag, handing it over the counter. This was the awkward part: As the son of her dad's best friend, as her sort-of neighbor, and as a public figure in the town, did he expect free food? They'd considered each other cousins when they were kids, and he liked to bring that up at awkward times. Sometimes he paid; sometimes he didn't, and she was never sure which a particular day would hold. She was just glad he didn't come by more than a few times a month.

Her stomach unclenched a little as he handed her a crisp five, and she smiled and gave him his change, as well as a coffee, black with one sugar, exactly like his dad had liked. "On the house," she said. She could afford that much for the sake of peace, at least.

He leaned in conspiratorially. "I hear you're starting a fight with those tech people," he said. "Let me know if you need advice. I've kept them out of our town for years now."

Marianne tried not to laugh. Tech startups speckled the area, including Swanley, and CoffeeGuru straddled the border with Wilshire. Its address was only technically in Wilshire because the front entrance happened to be on the Wilshire side. It was even *called* Wilshire-Swanley Tech Campus. Not to mention all the Airbnbs and the scooters people could rent on their phone that were cluttering the sidewalks. "Thank you," she said instead. "But we're figuring it out."

"I can count on your vote in the special election next month, can't I?"

"Of course."

He took a long look at her, long enough that she had to fight the urge to shift on her feet like a naughty child and then nodded. "Well, good luck to you."

"You too," she said, somewhat mystified. She watched him as he left, getting back into the BMW he'd parked illegally in front of the building; of course, his cousin was the Chief of Police, so he wasn't going to get a ticket anyway.

Now she really hoped he wasn't going to win. She didn't need to be represented in the state house by someone she was sure was up to no good.

The man had been family once, or near enough to it. She remembered building LEGO towns with him when they were in elementary school, forced together by their fathers' friendship. But he'd always been pushy and grasping, always stretching rules and breaking promises even then. That didn't seem to bother the folks with big money in the district—Marianne figured he probably kept most of the promises they bought from him. And what did he charge all these people for his special favors? Just a seat in the state government. Not too pricey. Not for the last time she wished Josh Robertson had turned down the governor's appointment. She knew Josh. She'd liked him. She'd voted for him all three times he'd run and won. He wasn't the brightest politician she'd ever met, and he didn't get much done as far as she could tell, but his heart was in the right place. She wasn't quite sure where Luke's was these days.

"That was weird." Zeke had come up behind her, arms crossed. "Wasn't that weird? He's never friendly."

"Sure was," said Marianne, shaking her head. "And he never stops by to chat. There's something going on with him."

*

"You would have thought we'd have gotten somewhere by now," Marianne complained to Rana a week later, shuffling papers on the counter as Doris, out of her postal uniform, and her wife Natasha dithered over which pie to buy. "It shouldn't be this difficult to find a property record."

"Maybe it's for the best," said Rana doubtfully. "If it's city property, do we want to have everyone know? We'll never even get spots for ourselves if that's the case."

"I think we're going to go with the cherry," said Natasha, and Marianne pulled out a box to package it up. "Are you talking about your parking lot? The one that's always filled up back there?"

"We've been wondering who's been parking there," said Doris. "I used to park my truck back there while delivering the area, but I can never get a spot anymore. Commuters?"

Marianne sighed. "Sort of. A new start-up has a carpool van that picks up across the street. We want to kick them out, but it's been harder than we thought."

Natasha winced in sympathy. "Took us years to get that sign on our corner. Remember, sweetie?"

"We just wanted a sign saying not to block our driveway," Doris explained. "Cars would park so close we could barely back out." She handed Marianne a twenty and took the pie. "Good luck with the traffic folks. They're something else."

Marianne followed them to the door, locking the deadbolt behind them and flipping the sign to Closed. Then she untied her apron and took a moment to unwind her customer service persona from around her.

Marianne's favorite time of her workday, clichéd as it sounded, was right after closing time. That's when she and Zeke cleaned the tables, debriefed, and got a moment out of the public eye. It might seem a little sad to outsiders that her closest companion was a seventeen-year-old kid, but after two years working together, they understood each other. Lately Rana had been stopping by a few days a week to chat while she closed between lunch and dinner, and she'd fit right in once she'd bullied Marianne into letting her help pack up the leftover pastries for Zeke's house, Marianne's apartment, and the VA or the shelter. But tonight, Zeke informed them early he had a special surprise for after closing. Marianne hoped she wasn't going to have to confiscate another Tupperware of "special" brownies from the kid—her patience for teen antics only went so far.

"Ta-da!" Zeke pulled a stiff, laminated piece of board from his oversized bag and brandished it. "Ready to go!"

Marianne laughed with delight, exchanging a glance with Rana, whose smile was slightly more reserved. "Nicely done!"

Zeke beamed, his usual teenage chill gone. "Can we hang it?"

"I don't see why not!" Marianne pulled out a bottle of construction glue and headed toward the back door, Rana and Zeke close behind her. Together, they held the sign up to the brick and glued the edges down firmly against the wall, where the words were easily visible to anyone entering the parking lot.

Customers Only. No Commuter Parking.

"Not bad," said Rana. "It looks real."

Zeke looked offended, running a hand over his springy black twists and gesturing toward the wall. "Looks real? It's a real sign!"

Marianne stepped back, hands on her hips. "Now it's just whether anyone will notice it."

Chapter Seven

Her question was answered in less than a day, with a visit from Officer Michael Blake of the Swanley Police Department.

"I'm sorry, Ms. Windmere," he said apologetically. "But that's not an authorized sign."

"How did you even hear about it?"

The officer paused, looking sheepish. "Well, ma'am, the chief's daughter started working at CoffeeGuru. There were complaints, and I guess she passed them along to her dad."

"Are you serious?" Marianne groaned. "Come on, Mickey. They're using my whole lot, and nobody's doing anything about it! It's driving business into the ground! Can't you give them tickets instead?"

Officer Blake shook his head, voice turning informal, back to the kid Marianne had babysat when she was a teen. "I'm sorry, Marianne. I wish I could help. I do. But you know how the chief is."

"So, what, we have to take it down?"

He winced. "And I have to fine you."

"A fine? That's absurd! The city won't give me an authorized sign! They won't even tell me if I'm authorized to *get* a sign!"

"And that's why they're making me fine you," said Michael. "I guess they told you no, and you did it anyway. That's what the chief said. He's not too happy with you."

He shook his head. "It's actually kind of weird how mad he is. Usually permitting isn't something he cares about."

"So, it's a permit problem?" She pointed at the porch she'd had installed a few years earlier. "I didn't need a permit to add that on, but for a two-foot sign I do?"

"The porch isn't the issue here. That's zoning, not traffic. Besides, Kevin probably eased that along. But any signage needs to be approved by the city." His voice was firmer, edging on annoyed.

Marianne took a long slow breath. It wouldn't do her any good to make Michael angry; he'd been a good kid when he was six and when he babysat her youngest back when he was thirteen and wanted to be a veterinarian when he grew up. But he was a cop now, and that was different. Thirty years of genial goodwill would only get her so far. "Okay," she said. "Give me the ticket. I'll take the sign down tonight."

He smiled, relieved. "Great. Thanks for cooperating, Ms. Windmere." He scribbled on his pad and handed her the page. "See you around. And give the kids my best if you talk to them."

"I will." She ushered him out and retreated to her office, where she sat heavily in her desk chair.

*

Marianne had just served scones to a nice old couple visiting from Florida when the door slammed open.

"What the hell, Marianne!" Kevin burst through the entry, heedless of the customers all turning to stare at him. "What do you think you're getting yourself into?"

"Calm down," said Marianne. "You're scaring the customers."

"I—" Kevin paused, took a deep breath through his nose, and glanced around at the half-filled cafe. The elderly couple was staring at him, the woman appalled, the man confused. "Fine. Can I talk to you in private, please?"

Marianne sighed. "Zeke, can you cover the counter for a few minutes?"

"Sure, boss." Zeke gave Kevin a wide berth. He'd never liked Kevin—of course, he'd been five when they'd divorced, so he'd never known them as a couple. And Kevin seemed to particularly annoy him. She thought perhaps Kevin's predilection for grandstanding and self-promotion, or maybe his deep-held belief that only he could save the town of Swanley from any problems that came up were the cause. Deep down, Kevin considered himself Swanley's best and only native son, despite the fact that his roots in the town only went two generations deep to Zeke's at least five. Marianne wasn't quite sure what the precise reason was, but she trusted Zeke to make his own choices about who he liked and didn't like, especially about straight white men.

She kind of wished she'd known somebody like Zeke when she was sixteen. He'd have talked her out of marrying Kevin real quick. Or maybe it was that he'd worked for Marianne part-time for the last few years and, unlike most of the town, knew her side of the story much better than Kevin's. She appreciated the support from him and his great-grandfather regardless of the cause.

She gestured to Kevin to follow her behind the counter and into the back office where she plopped down into her grandfather's big leather chair.

"You could have asked me!" Kevin burst out as soon as the door shut behind them. "Why wouldn't you ask me for help with this? I could have fixed this if you'd let me! I could have gotten it all figured out without getting the whole town government's panties in a twist!"

Marianne ran a frustrated hand through her hair. "Kevin, you're not on the city council anymore. And besides, it's none of your business what I do. I don't recall asking you for help. All I'm trying to do is to get my parking lot reserved for *my* customers."

"And you're pissing off the chief of police as well as the assessor's office in the process! Do you know how embarrassing it is for me when my ex-wife goes rogue and starts hanging unapproved signs around town?"

"Around town? It was on my building, Kevin! And besides, you don't need to worry about your reputation anymore! Isn't that what you said when you retired? That you could wear socks and sandals, and it wouldn't be front page news?"

"That's different!"

"And you're not my husband anymore either. Remember? We're divorced. And that was your idea, if I recall, after your last conference in Schenectady and that mayor's aide? You said something about needing the freedom to live your life?" Marianne thought that maybe she was being unfair, but she didn't care. The words felt too good coming out.

"Well, maybe the divorce was a mistake."

Marianne stared at him. "Really? Now you want to do this?"

He crossed his arms over his chest, looking uncomfortable, like he might bolt at any minute. "Do what?"

"We didn't work together, and you know it. We only stayed married as long as we did because of the kids, and because we never saw each other long enough to get on each other's nerves."

"I still love you!"

"No, you don't." Marianne ran a hand through her hair and closed her eyes for a moment to gather her thoughts. She didn't want to be having this conversation, and she didn't want to ever have it again. "Kevin, I know you. Okay, maybe you love me. But you don't want to be married to me any more than I want to be married to you. I want you in my life, but not as a spouse. Not after everything we've been through." She laid a hand on his elbow. "You always want what you can't have." She shook her head. "I don't need you to fight my battles for me anymore. And actually, I never did."

"Anna says you're seeing someone."

"I might be." He didn't need to know things with Rana probably wouldn't go anywhere.

"Who? Do I know him? Her? Them?"

Marianne appreciated the correction, but not enough to give him any more information he didn't need. "That's none of your business, Kevin." She reached out and patted his shoulder. "And don't act like you haven't dated. I know you've made the rounds at the PTA—you've dated a few graduating classes worth of moms, at this point."

At this, Kevin looked even more uncomfortable, not meeting her eyes.

"We're friends. I like that." She took his hand, trying to get him to relax a little from his tension. "But there are boundaries."

"And nepotism in city government is your limit?" He was regaining his composure now; having realized the playacting wasn't going to work, he made an effort to drop his practiced affect.

These were the moments she still loved him, a little: the moments when she saw the man he could have been underneath all the posturing and grandstanding. She hadn't seen much of that man while they were married, just enough to keep her hoping for more. She'd never been able to coax that Kevin to the surface for long, and in the last few years, watching her kids struggle to find people to spend their lives with she'd realized her mistake. She would never have been able to fix the damage an upbringing as a man in the 1960s had done to a guy more interested in rom-coms and debate club than football and fights. Years of his parents telling him to act like a man and push down the feelings that sometimes overwhelmed him could only be fixed by Kevin himself, ideally with the professional help of a therapist. Marianne wondered if he'd ever talked to one. She hoped so. But aging seemed to be doing what a lifetime of people telling him he could have his way—and what that way should be—hadn't. It was teaching him humility, and maybe making the whole act more tiring than being honest.

"Pretty much." She shook her head. "I appreciate that you want to help. But this is my problem, and I'll figure it out."

He sighed, the annoyance draining from his shoulders, and squeezed her hand. "You've changed, you know that? You're tougher than you used to be. I need to get used to that."

"I'm not sure if that's a compliment," she observed. "But yes, you need to."

"And I'll step back. But you had better believe I'll be watching out for you if you have to fight for whatever you're trying to do. And anything you need that I can do, I'll do."

"I'd expect no less from an old friend and neighbor."

"And that's all I am to you?"

"That's worth quite a bit, don't you think?"

Kevin smiled, and it was genuine this time, sweet, and a little tired. "I guess it is."

Marianne, seeing that real familiar smile, considered for a moment giving in and asking him to intercede on her behalf at city hall. He'd say yes in an instant, thrilled to have a chance to flex his connections and waning power in the town and maybe gain back a little of her goodwill. But that would bring him inside the neat little space she'd carved out with Rana, the delicate balance of the project that had brought them together after pushing them apart. And even though he probably could help, she didn't want him to. She didn't want to involve anyone else. She and Rana would solve this together, and then who knows what would happen. They didn't need help. "I do appreciate the offer," she said because she really did. "I have to figure this out on my own."

He gave in. "I know. But just know—there might be more going on here than you think. Just be careful."

"I'm always careful, Kevin." She opened the office door. "Let me handle this. After all, it's a sign. How hard can getting a sign be?"

He gave her a long look before striding back out of the office and through the store.

"Everything all right?" asked Zeke.

Marianne nodded, watching the door swing closed behind Kevin. "He doesn't like when stuff goes on in Swanley that he's not in charge of; that's all. I told him we had it covered."

Zeke snorted. "He must have been insufferable as a teenager."

Marianne raised an eyebrow. "You know I married him when he was nineteen, right?"

"Hey, everybody makes mistakes."

Marianne snorted. "You've got that right, Zeke."

*

The bell over the door sounded as Marianne finished a spiral of whipped cream on the caramel soy latte for the older man at the corner table. The espresso machine had been acting up lately, and she kept one eye on it for leaks and drips as she drizzled chocolate syrup over the top. Out of the corner of her eye, she saw someone making their way up to the register. "Just a minute," she sang over her shoulder and then hustled to the counter to call out the drink. By the time she'd turned back around, Rana had set a plate of tiny cheese turnovers—the ones Marianne had loved so much the first time she'd met Rana—next to Marianne's own coffee on the counter and was smiling at her from in front of the register. "Oh! Hi," said Marianne, hurrying back to the counter. "I didn't expect to see you!"

"It's Tuesday," Rana explained. "I close early, but I stay a bit later to prep for the week sometimes. I need to catch up from my Monday off." That dimple appeared back in her cheek, and Marianne felt her own cheeks redden.

I'm fifty-eight years old! She scolded herself as she smiled apologetically and handed the drink to its rightful owner. *I cannot be blushing like a schoolgirl in the middle of my bakery!*

"I hope you don't mind," said Rana hesitantly, the dimple fading. "I thought you liked these last time."

"I did!" said Marianne hurriedly, automatically reaching out to grab Rana's wrist to stop her leaving.

"Sorry, it's been a long day. Thank you so much." She glanced at the display case. "I've got one almond croissant left, and I think this was a particularly good batch. Do you have a moment for a quick snack?"

Rana's smile returned full force. "I always have time for a snack." She glanced around. "But don't you need to attend to your customers?"

"Zeke should be back from his break in a few minutes," said Marianne. "And besides, everybody knows me. If anyone comes in, they'll pester me until I serve them. Here." She set the plate with the croissant beside Rana's, admiring the contrast between her pink-and-white-flowered china and Rana's blue-and-red-patterned ones. They looked good together. She swallowed hard, fighting the smitten grin that was trying to claw its way out. "Would you like a drink? Coffee? Tea?"

"Oh, no, thank you." Rana settled in the chair, a few tendrils of hair escaping the heavy bun at the nape of her neck to frame her face. She glanced up at Marianne, meeting her eyes. "Thank you for the croissant." Her low even voice and light accent cut through the chatter of the bakery easily. "I had an odd encounter this morning, and I wanted your opinion on it."

Marianne paused with a sambousik halfway to her mouth. She set it back down. "What kind of encounter?"

Rana shook her head. "My landlord came by."

"Is that unusual?" Marianne gave in and bit into the sambousik. The warm cheese had exactly the right balance of spice and salt, and she nearly moaned at its flavor. "He came by here last week looking for votes."

Rana smiled, watching her as she chewed. "It is. He visits rarely, and he's never brought anyone along with him. That was the odd part."

"Who did he have with him?"

"I'm not sure who they were, but they were in suits and they had a long quiet discussion. Then they stood in the parking lot for a long time, pointing at the building. I thought perhaps they were contractors here to make repairs or redo the façade, but if that were it, he would have introduced them, wouldn't he?"

"That seems right," said Marianne. She didn't like the sound of this, not one bit. "I mean, he could be doing some work on the property. It doesn't have to be nefarious."

"You've known him far longer than I have. Does that seem likely?"

Marianne sighed. "No, it doesn't. Even with his new running-for-office facelift, he's the same scumbag he's always been." She leaned back in her chair, glancing out the window toward Rana's half of the building. "I don't like it."

Rana made a sudden noise of surprise and Marianne turned to look at her. She held the croissant in one hand and stared at it, her other hand over her mouth.

"Are you all right?"

Her cheeks darkened, her eyes wide, she flicked her gaze from the pastry to Marianne. "This is incredible," she said, swallowing. "Oh my goodness, Marianne, this croissant!"

Marianne laughed as the bell over the door rang, announcing a customer. She stood to go help the girl who'd just walked in, grabbing another sambousik for the trip back to the counter. "Thank you for the snack," she said, wondering if there was a way to politely ask Rana to stick around for the next couple hours so they could have dinner together and hating the nervousness that kept her from being able to *ask*. "It was delicious."

"I'll be over at the store," said Rana. "If you'd like to have dinner later."

Marianne's heart lightened. "I'd love that."

Rana nodded and slipped out the door. Marianne watched her go until the teen in front of her cleared his throat. "Ma'am?" he asked. "Um, can we order?"

Flustered, she flicked the espresso machine back on. From the other side of the counter, Zeke snorted as he tied his apron on. "Boss," he said, voice low. "You're worse than I am with a crush."

"Oh yeah," she retorted just as quietly as they passed each other at the cake fridge, "wait until Doris comes by with the mail. We'll see who's more embarrassing then."

"That's a low blow, boss lady," said Zeke, hand over his heart. "And rude." He pointed at her. "Just for that, I'm taking my break the minute coupon lady comes in. Watch me."

She couldn't find it in her gleeful heart to give him any more trouble.

Chapter Eight

The next day a sign posted on Rana's door caught Marianne's eye as she walked back from the pharmacy with her prescription in hand. She stopped on the sidewalk to check it out. "Closed until Saturday for vacation," she read. "Huh." Rana hadn't said anything about going anywhere, but then, she didn't have to. They were neighbors, and maybe friends. Marianne's heart sank at the thought of no casual dinners or shared coffee for a week. *I really am in this deep. Zeke was right. What am I doing?* She'd missed her shot with Rana—she knew that. All she could hope for now was friendship, which was wonderful on its own. She didn't need more than that. She really didn't.

She waited a moment and then continued toward her own door, heart a little heavier. She wondered where Rana had gone, whether it was back home to Egypt or somewhere else. She'd have to ask on Tuesday, if she saw her.

"Here she comes now," Zeke was saying as she entered. The bakery was half full, the tables mostly occupied, and a very short line at the register consisted of a couple locals. She smiled at Zeke, whose face had a dash of panic across it. He didn't like handling crowds alone, even crowds filled with people he'd known all his life.

"Sorry, Zeke," she said, tucking her pharmacy bag and purse under the counter, nearly knocking over the row of small wooden nutcrackers Zeke had lined up on top of the display case. "How can I help you?" She asked the customer in front of the register and then gasped. "Rana! I thought you were away!"

Rana looked more relaxed than Marianne had seen her—anytime except after their kiss, that is—and had an arm around a tall woman who shared Rana's smooth olive-brown skin and long nose. The corners of her eyes were barely sprinkled with the laugh lines that Rana had in abundance, and her dimple sat on the opposite cheek from Rana's. "Nour, this is my very good friend Marianne." She turned that megawatt, dimpled smile on Marianne, who ducked her head, feeling herself blush at the description.

"You must be Rana's daughter," said Marianne, shaking her head. She imagined Rana must have looked like this in her thirties, minus Nour's stylish, thick-rimmed glasses and headscarf. Although maybe Rana had worn the hijab when she'd lived in Egypt. Marianne wondered if that would be a rude question to ask sometime when they were alone. "Welcome!"

"It's wonderful to meet you," said Nour. "My mother has told me so much about you. But we should let the other customers order, Mamti." Her accent was lighter than Rana's, the barest hint on the occasional word, and Marianne recalled that this was the daughter who'd been born in Egypt and had only spent a few years in the US before moving back.

Rana laughed, squeezing her around the waist. "Always looking out for others, that's my little girl. Marianne, perhaps we could have dinner tomorrow? I wanted to show Nour around town, but I'd love to spend some time introducing you two without all the customers."

"My mother wants to prove to me she's making friends," said Nour. "We didn't believe her."

"Nour!" Rana's cheeks darkened. "My daughter is very rude."

"So are you," said Ray from behind them. "I thought you liked your customers. We're not invited out to dinner?"

Rana laughed again. "I do like my customers, but I like Marianne better. I'm sorry, Ray, but it's true."

Marianne's stomach fluttered.

"Even my wife likes Marianne better than me," Ray admitted. "I get it. I'd like her better than me, too, when she's baking."

Marianne grinned at him. "Compliment me all you like, but you're not getting me to make peach pie until the summer." Her smile softened when she turned back to Rana. "I'd love dinner," she said. "Would you like a coffee, or a treat? On the house?"

"Oh, no, thank you," said Rana. "We're taking the train into Boston for dinner with an old friend of our family. But we'll see you tomorrow?"

"I wouldn't miss it," Marianne reassured her and then waved as they left, arm in arm.

Ray raised his eyebrows as he stepped up to the counter. "Well."

"What?" She snapped.

"Oh, nothing." He grinned. "Do your kids know you've gone back to fourteen years old? You're worse than my Krissy."

Marianne looked at the ceiling hopelessly. "Not you too," she said.

"Relax," he said, his voice kind. "I'm glad you're getting back out there."

"I'm not, really. We aren't—it's not like we're dating or anything. I'm making friends."

"Well, I don't look at most of my friends that way."

"Maybe your friends aren't as pretty!" she snapped.

Ray held up his hands in surrender. "All right, all right," he said, laughing. "Then I'm glad you're making new *friends*. And I'm glad you're burying the hatchet with that storefront. We all had bets on when you'd finally give in and give a restaurant over there a try."

"Oh yeah? Who won the bet?"

"Nobody. The last bet was for 2013, so I think we all lost fair and square."

Marianne handed him his coffee and decided not to tell him that particular hatchet was well and truly unburied.

*

As she locked the door and flicked off the lights in the seating area, Marianne called out to Zeke, who was beginning to rinse trays in the sink. "Do you want to earn some overtime tonight?"

He looked up, suspicious. "You're not going to ask me to clean the grease traps again, are you? Because that requires, like, *triple* overtime."

She laughed. "No, and after last time, it's not worth asking you again. I'd rather do it myself than listen to you complain that much again."

"Mission accomplished." He crossed his arms. "I try not to pick up that learned helplessness man thing as I work on my butch, but, uh, I'll keep it up for things that gross."

"I promise, it isn't food-related! And it shouldn't be gross. At least, I don't think so."

"Okay, I'm interested. I do need some extra cash for Joe's Christmas present." He grinned. "Getting him a Kindle so he can make all his books large print. I'm tired of him leaving magnifiers and book lights all over the house."

"I hope that present includes lessons and a set-up day," Marianne said, impressed with the thoughtfulness. "Because you know Joe. He's not big on technology. But that sounds like a great idea."

"They're pretty intuitive," said Zeke. "And I'm off from school the week you're closed here, so I can load his books on, and then we can spend some time working on it."

"Okay, well, I'm thinking we might need a couple hours for the project I'm thinking of. We don't have to do it all tonight, but I was hoping to go through some of the file cabinets, and I need your help and your young eyes."

"Now *you* sound like Joe." He looked intrigued. "Okay, yeah, that sounds kind of cool. Even the one that's been there for ages? The wooden one?"

"I don't think anyone's opened that one since my dad died," she admitted. "It's probably the best place to start."

"What are we looking for?"

She shrugged. "I'm not quite sure. The deed to the property, for sure. Anything with a map. We'll probably know what we're looking for once we find it."

He nodded decisively. "I'll get the Swiffer. The top of that thing's so dusty we'll have to wear masks if we don't clean it first."

She nodded and led the way upstairs, sizing up the filing cabinets along the wall of her office, grabbed a can of wood cleaner, then started getting to work on the front and sides as Zeke cleaned the top. Together they tugged the whole thing out to the center of the office. "I have no idea what's inside," she admitted. "I know my dad tried to keep files while Grandpa was training him, but my grandfather always told him he was doing it wrong, and I think once he took over my dad kind of gave up on being very organized. And who knows if Simon even kept any records." She waved at the other, more modern cabinet. "I know he put taxes in there, but other than that, I'm not sure. I've got my own files downstairs—when I took over, I figured it'd be easier to start fresh."

"Only one way to find out," said Zeke, tugging the top drawer open and peering inside. "Looks like it's not even in files," he said. "Just dusty, dusty piles. We might want to clear off the table."

Marianne got to work. First, she pushed her loose recipe cards all into a box and set it on her desk and then cleared off the pile of her kids' old macaroni art and report cards to set them on a chair. She winced at the thought of how long it had been since she'd cleaned the office. Her youngest, Jacob, was twenty-four. That made this pile old enough to enroll in college.

"Okay." Zeke snapped on a pair of latex gloves. "What?" he said in response to her look. "Dust dries my skin out. I don't look this good by *accident*, you know."

Marianne smothered a smile.

Zeke shook his head and grabbed a pile of paper and set it on one corner and then handed her another. "You're hopeless. Want to start sorting?"

"Let's put stuff that's obviously trash right in the recycling," she said and pulled the bin closer. "So any old vendor receipts, order forms, stuff like that from before my time, unless it's more than fifty years old or you recognize the name. And anything that looks important, put it over here." She waved to her desk chair. "We'll go through that once we've gotten the nonsense out."

He nodded. "And if I find any dirty letters, I'll make a separate pile that you don't get to see."

Marianne threw a Swiffer pad at him, and Zeke ducked, laughing.

They sorted for an hour or so, finding nothing particularly interesting, but plenty that Marianne put aside. She had a dream of someday writing a book or running some kind of blog about the history of the bakery. Maybe for an anniversary or something, though they'd not done much for the hundredth, which had happened while Luke Leventi's father Simon was running things. Another mark against that family, she thought, though she knew that was perhaps not a reasonable thing to be angry about.

"I don't trust him," admitted Marianne, passing over another pile of receipts for the recycling bin as she picked up the thread of conversation that had trailed off five minutes earlier. She was glad she'd asked Zeke to help, both for her sake and for his. For his because she knew that Joe was living on social security and couldn't afford to support his great-grandson without any help from Zeke's parents, let alone cover the cost of his testosterone and eventual surgery. He had a fundraiser online, she knew, but most of the people donating seemed to be other young trans kids essentially returning the money he'd donated to their own healthcare. None of them could afford much. She'd made donations when she could, but anything she could pay him to do around the shop helped. And this was for her benefit, too, because she knew if she were doing this project by herself, or with one of her kids, she'd be stopping to read every page, reminiscing and mourning her father and mother and grandfather all over again. Instead, she and Zeke were moving quickly, already through the first drawer and onto the second, with a pile only a few inches high of stuff to keep.

"Mr. Leventi?" Zeke looked up from the pile. "Why not?" He smiled. "Well, I mean, I know why not generally—because he's a sleazeball—but why specifically now? What did he do?"

"That's the thing," said Marianne. "I don't know what he's up to." She sighed. "I liked it better when he ignored the place except to get rent."

"You like his tenant better now though."

"Well, that's true."

"Maybe he's hanging around Rana to try to get a date?"

Marianne shook a finger at Zeke. "Don't even think that. Get me a new pile—I'm not paying you to tease me about the cute neighbor."

He raised an eyebrow. "So, you *do* think she's cute."

She groaned. "Of course, I do! Come on, you have to admit she's a good-looking woman. But I'm not trying to date anybody, Zeke. Now can we get back to work?"

He laughed as he headed back around the cabinet to dig out another pile of folders. At least in this drawer everything was hung instead of sitting in a crumpled, dusty stack.

"Hey, is this it?" asked Zeke, his short twists poking up from behind the file cabinet the only part of him Marianne could see from her seat. "Hey, boss, holy crap, I think this might be what we're looking for!" He stood, stepping carefully over the piles of papers on the floor. Marianne spun in her chair as he approached, rubbing dust from her face with a rag. Even the hanging folders were soaked in dust.

"What did you find?"

"Looks like a folder from your dad. That's his writing, right?"

"In 1969," read Marianne. "You might be right." She tried not to get her hopes up. No matter what she found, a lot of work stood before her. If the deed said she owned the lot, that was great and would solve one problem, but the official border with Rana's property was still up in the air. If the documentation said she didn't have rights to the lot—well, she'd cross that bridge if it came to it. She opened the folder.

A pile of yellowing papers fell out onto the table, their musty smell filling the air. Zeke perched on the stool beside her, intrigued. "Look at this!" He pulled out a photograph, black and white with a thick white border on heavy paper. "It looks exactly the same." He was right. The photo showed the bakery, circa 1948, according to the note on the back. The brick was the same, the letters freshly painted on the windows, and the sidewalk neatly swept. The only thing missing was the porch.

Marianne stared at the man in the suit and the teenage boy beside him, both staring seriously into the camera; her father and her grandfather in front of the bakery that was both of their lives and already a family institution for a generation when the photo was taken. She tried to see her son Jacob in the faces of the two men standing on the stoop. There was Anna's nose and her own wide-set eyes, but none of her children had the distinctive Windmere fair coloring and thin frame her father and grandfather shared.

"Why do you think they sold it?" asked Zeke. "I mean, that's what we're trying to find out, right?"

"Well, my grandfather was long gone by then," said Marianne. "And my father—the war changed him, Zeke. Just like a lot of guys. And I don't know...he had me to raise, and my mother was sick. Maybe he felt like it was too much for him to handle." She picked up a page and began to try to piece out the worn cursive. "'Bounded northerly by the water known as Crow Creek for fifty-seven feet, northeasterly by the land of F. P. Nottingham eighty-six feet, easterly by the cliffs forty-nine feet...' This might be a copy of the original deed to the property. Wow, Zeke, this is amazing!"

"Your family's had it that long?" asked Zeke, leaning over her shoulder. "Since when?"

"The property? Since 1866," said Marianne. "My great-great-grandfather Marvelle bought the land with his bonus when he came home from the war. Then his son Talmadge turned it into the bakery."

"The Civil War?" asked Zeke. "He fought?"

"All the men in the town did pretty much right from the beginning," said Marianne.

"All the white men, you mean," Zeke corrected. "I know the black guys didn't get to fight until late in the war."

"You're right," said Marianne. "Joe's granddad fought, right?"

Zeke smiled. "Joseph Green. Family hero. His mom's dad who'd escaped North Carolina with his mom a few years before the war. Grampa knew him, he says, and he says he's named after him. He died when Grampa was nine. That's why he made sure we knew about him."

"Well, I know he knew my great-granddad a long time," said Marianne. "All the men who came home stuck together, I think. They'd seen things the rest of the town didn't understand. Guess that made for strong bonds. It's probably part of why my grandfather hired Joe."

"Your dad had the VA for that, right? Which is why we bring them our leftovers?"

"That's right. Although there weren't nearly as many after Vietnam as there were after World War II," Marianne sighed. "Maybe if there'd been more vets around when Dad came back, things might have been different." She carefully gathered the pile of crackly paper, tucking it into a folder. "I wonder if this means anything to the assessor anymore. I know Crow Creek's been gone for a century, and the cliffs got mined out years ago and flattened. It used to be where that condo development is now, on that hill."

Zeke handed her the photo and a manila envelope secured with a piece of string. "What's this?"

"I don't know," said Marianne. "Let me see." Zeke handed her the folder. It had some heft, and the scattering of dust along the flap made her think it hadn't been opened in a while. She unwound the twine carefully, folding the flap back.

It was filled with pages and photos, all scattered and disarrayed. She pulled out a photo first and gave a little gasp. Her mother and her father stared out from the white frame, standing in front of the old cast-iron stove in the bakery—a shot she'd never seen before. Her father's hand rested on her mother's belly and both smiled. Her mother's bright grin was directed at the camera, but her father's was smaller, sweeter, and only directed at his wife. They looked so young. She'd never seen his face look so open in a picture as an adult; happy and without the shadow the war and her mother's death would bring to his face. And her mother looked beautiful, glowing. Marianne ached, remembering what little she could of her. She swallowed hard and set the photo aside carefully. She'd frame it, maybe hang it in the bakery. She thought her dad would have liked that.

Beneath that was a stack of graph paper stapled in the corner and folded haphazardly in half. She picked the sheets up and pressed them flat. "Last Will and Testament of Daniel Windmere," read Zeke from over her shoulder. "Wait. That's your dad."

Marianne stared at the document. "This can't be."

"Why not?"

"My dad didn't leave a will. His property all went to probate and to me eventually, but the process was a whole ordeal because there wasn't a will."

"I mean, this might say otherwise." Zeke reached out and put a hand on her shoulder. "Hey, are you okay, boss?"

Marianne relaxed her grip on the paper, her eyes tracing the familiar lines of her father's signature. "Dated 1969," she read at the bottom. "November. He was only back from Vietnam a year when this was written." She shook her head. "This was when my mom was sick." She smoothed it out, lifting the first page gently. "I was almost ten."

""What does it say?" asked Zeke. "Do you want to read it?"

"I don't know," said Marianne. "I don't know if I can."

"Do you want me to read it to you?"

Marianne looked up. Zeke's brows were drawn together, concern evident in his round face. He'd grown up so much in the couple of years since he'd transitioned, and the changes weren't from the T. He'd metamorphosed from a kid she gave a job to as a favor to Joe into someone she trusted and relied upon. When had he grown up?

"I'd like that," she said. "Thanks, Zeke." She leaned back as he started to read, hesitating a little over some of the messier words and let her father's ghost wash over her. It sounded like him, even in Zeke's lighter, younger voice. The words had his particular cadence. There were no real surprises in the first few pages. Her mother would get everything, and if her mother died, she would, with one exception.

"In the event that I am incapacitated and my daughter Marianne Windmere is not yet twenty-five at the time of my death, and my wife Helena has predeceased me, Simon Leventi shall be granted conservatorship over the property at 121 Main Street known as Windmere Bakery, as well as any tenants they may hold in any part of the property, commercial or residential, to continue his management of the building and business, until such time as Marianne Windmere requests control returned to her. He is not authorized to alter Windmere Bakery in any form without the written approval of Marianne Windmere or her heir. In payment, he shall be granted 25% of the profits from all enterprises conducted therein during his time as conservator."

"Well, that makes sense," said Marianne. "That's what happened after he died. I let Simon run it for years before I came back to the business."

"What about the other side?" asked Zeke. "Did he run that too? Because it says that thing about commercial tenants. You've never had tenants down here, have you?"

Marianne frowned. "Let me see that?"

Zeke handed her the will.

She skimmed the page, flipping it to read the next one. "He never says it's just suite A," she said. "That's strange. This would have been immediately after he sold it. I think. I would have thought he would clarify that in a legal document."

"Huh." Zeke shook his head. "That sounds like the start of a really boring episode of *Law and Order*."

"More like the middle," admitted Marianne. "At least a TV show would have a murder at the start. We're trapped in file cabinets forever."

Zeke laughed and handed her another stack. "We're almost to the bottom of this drawer though. Want to see what other mysteries we can find?"

She pushed her filthy sleeves back up to her elbows. "Lead on."

Chapter Nine

After a busy day of customers, Marianne had expected a quiet meal in Rana's restaurant with Rana and her daughter. But when Rana showed up at her door after closing time, she was wearing a coat and a dress. "We made reservations at Masala," she said, voice a little nervous. "I hope you don't mind. Our treat."

Marianne looked down at her flour-coated apron and the casual clogs she wore for her long days in the bakery. "I hope you can wait twenty minutes for me to change."

"Of course!" Rana nodded. "We'll be in our restaurant when you're ready. The reservation isn't until six."

Marianne nodded and hurried inside. She could clean up the bakery later—she'd done most of the work already, just a few big pans to wash and the napkin dispensers to refill. They could wait a few hours. She glanced down at her watch—4:50. If she hurried, she could squeeze in a shower and let a dress hang in the bathroom to steam out the wrinkles.

She looked pretty good, she decided, for fifty-eight and a ten-hour workday. The deep-blue dress had a neckline that showed off the shoulders she'd earned through years of kneading dough while still maintaining some dignity, and the tea length let her show off the black leather boots Janie had helped her pick out the previous December. Apparently, they were very *in*. And the peacoat Anna had given her a few years earlier fit over the top nicely, she decided as she checked herself out in the hall mirror. Yes, this look would do nicely for this—whatever the occasion was.

It wasn't a date, not with Rana's daughter along. A nice dinner out; that was all. If they'd kept up what they'd started that night of the storm—but they hadn't. They wouldn't. She'd missed her chance, and that was probably a good thing. Marianne didn't do well with relationships, generally; she knew she had trouble distinguishing attraction from wanting friendship, and when the feelings struck this sudden and this hard the uncertainty made her all the more nervous. Rana made her feel all of sixteen again, all nerves and elbows.

But they were both nearing sixty, grown women, and they were friends. Rana wanted to be friends; Marianne knew that much. And she liked Rana, wanted to spend time with her. It had been a long time since Marianne had made a new friend. She smiled, tucked her wallet in her purse, and headed down the stairs and around the building to the other suite.

Rana and Nour sat together in a Cairo Grill booth, leaning over a cell phone, their faces lit by the glow of the screen. Marianne was struck once again by how similar the two looked.

"Hi," she said, letting the door swing closed behind her. "Am I late?"

Rana looked up, staring at Marianne for a long moment before smiling. "Oh, no, not at all! Nour, are you ready?"

"Whenever you are," said Nour, gathering her things. "I've been craving Indian food, American style. You can't get the same kinds in Egypt."

"There's no Indian food there?" Marianne asked as they started down the sidewalk toward the center of town. "I would have thought there would be more. You're much closer than we are."

Nour smiled. "Oh, there's plenty. Authentic too. But I missed the American kind. It's less like what you find in India, but it's its own delicious cuisine."

"My daughter Janie's girlfriend is Chinese," offered Marianne. "Or at least her parents are. She says when she goes to China, she loves her grandmother's cooking, but she misses her General Tso's. I guess that's the same thing."

Rana laughed. "I can't believe that's what people call Chinese food here." She pushed open the door to the restaurant. "I'm doing my best to keep my food somewhat like what you'd find in Cairo."

"I keep telling you that you should branch out," said Nour. "Maybe some Moroccan dishes, some Lebanese. There's a market for it."

"Ah, Nour, you see, I don't want more customers."

"She's got plenty," Marianne added. "I keep telling her she needs to hire somebody."

Rana turned to Marianne. "And I keep telling *you*, if I hire someone, I won't trust that everything will get done the way I like it."

"Isn't not having to do it all worth having some of it done wrong?"

"No!" replied Nour and Rana at the same time. They looked at each other and laughed.

"Mamti says if you can't do it the right way, you have no business doing it. That's how my father got out of doing laundry his whole life," said Nour.

"He sounds like a smart man," Marianne replied as Rana checked in with the hostess, confirming their reservations. "I wish I'd met him."

Nour gave her a skeptical look, eyebrows nearly disappearing into her loose headscarf. "If my father were alive, you wouldn't be flirting with my mother this much, I hope."

"I'm not—" Marianne's brain stuttered for a moment, and when it let her back in, Nour and Rana were ten feet ahead of her following the hostess to their table. She forced herself to start walking again, catching up as the hostess pulled out Rana's chair. Nour gave her a wide, sneaky grin as she settled in her chair and picked up a papadum.

Marianne rarely went out to dinner, and she hadn't been to Masala in years. She hadn't been a lot of places in Swanley in years, she realized, looking around at the bustling restaurant.

"So," said Nour, opening the little pot of green mint chutney and spooning some onto her plate. "My mother says you've been neighbors for months but only just met. That doesn't seem very neighborly."

"Nour!" said Rana sharply. "That isn't polite."

Nour raised her hands. "Sorry, Marianne. I'm only curious. Why didn't you two meet earlier? You get along very well, so I can't imagine why."

Marianne sighed. "It's a fair question. And the answer is that I'm an idiot."

"Marianne!" Now it was Marianne that Rana's sharp Mom voice was directed at.

"It's true!" Marianne held up her hands. "Nour, the space your mother's shop occupies used to be part of my bakery. And there's a whole weird history around how it ended up *not* part of the bakery anymore. But either way, I've been taking out my anger at the strange situation on the people working there, rather than the people responsible." She turned toward Rana. "I don't know if I've ever apologized for that, by the way."

"You don't need to—"

"Yes, I do. For my own benefit. I do." Marianne pushed her hair behind her ears and then reached out and rested a hand on Rana's wrist. "I'm sorry, Rana. I was rude, and I shouldn't have been. I should have come by when you moved in, and I should have met you much sooner."

"I—" Rana met her eyes, lines in the corners crinkling as her cheeks flushed. "Thank you."

Marianne looked into those eyes for another moment, drinking in the warmth there and then cleared her throat. "Anyway." She pulled her hand back, curling it under the table to hold onto the heat of Rana's. "That's all I wanted to say."

"I approve," said Nour. "And I want pakora to celebrate."

"I won't disagree with that order," said Marianne, grateful for the break in emotional conversation.

The pakora were delicious, as always, brought by Charlie, a kid whose father had worked at the bakery as a custodian back before Marianne's father died. Marianne spent a moment catching up with him as Nour and Rana looked on, amused.

"What?" she asked after Charlie cleared their papadum plates. "His dad worked for my dad, right after the family came to the US. I've known that kid since before he was born."

"It's interesting," said Nour. "You know everyone in this town."

"Not everyone!" protested Marianne. "I didn't know you until recently, for example. Just the people who've been here my whole life. How could I not?"

Rana shook her head. "It's nice, in some ways. We've moved around since we came to this country, and we have people scattered across the globe. All of your community is right nearby."

"A little too nearby," said Marianne. "No privacy in this town." She glanced around. "In this room right now, I see two of my kids' teachers, three customers, and somebody who was a Boy Scout with my ex-husband. My second cousin was eating at PJ's next door with his girlfriend, whose ex-wife is the sister of our mail carrier. So, everybody knows everybody's business." She glanced around. "Eyes on your own soup, Frankie." A man two tables down who'd obviously been eavesdropping grinned, waved, and turned back to his conversation.

"That's how life is in our neighborhood back in Giza," said Nour thoughtfully. "I've lived there six years now, and everyone in the building watches out for one another."

"It's different there," said Rana. "You're in a city. You can go two blocks and be surrounded by strangers. It's not better or worse, but it's certainly a different experience than here. This is more like the village my mother grew up in. But at least now we have the internet and television." She shook her head. "The way she told it, the only entertainment they had was gossip."

"Oh, poor Jidda," said Nour, laughing a little. "She hated gossip."

"She got enough of it at home," said Rana.

"So, your family hasn't always lived in Cairo?" asked Marianne.

"Oh, goodness, no," Rana thanked Charlie as he set a steaming bowl of vindaloo in front of her. "My father comes from a town on the Libyan border. My mother is from a port town farther north. They both came to Cairo in the twenties looking for work. They met and fell in love in a linen factory." She smiled. "Nour, you remember visiting your grandmother's village."

"It's beautiful there," said Nour. "If you like desert and quiet." She laughed. "Not the ideal place for children used to movies and computers."

"It made my mother happy, though, to have us with her when she visited," said Rana. "Especially knowing she could go back to Cairo afterward."

Seeing Rana and her daughter together made Marianne's heart ache from missing her own kids—all three of them—scattered around the country. *At least they're all in the US. Nour's trip to see her mother is much farther.*

She resolved to give Janie a call, and Jacob, if he picked up, that evening. Anna was her communicator—they talked at least once a week, if not more—but her other two were harder to pin down. She missed her family. At least Kevin was nearby, complicated though that relationship would always be. He was family, divorce or no. They'd been through too much for too long for that not to be true.

"So, I'm curious," said Nour. "About this weird situation you mentioned with the Grill. Can I ask about it, or is that rude?"

"It's all right," said Marianne, glancing at Rana. "The building used to be all one business—my great-grandfather built the original house back in the 1800s with his father's Civil War pension. Then about eighty years later it wasn't doing so well after my dad came back from Vietnam, and he sold part of the building to his friend. That was your mother's landlord's father, Simon. And Simon ran the whole bakery, my part included, while I figured out my life. I took control back in the nineties, but Simon wasn't thrilled to give up control and it sort of caused a rift. And now we're trying to figure out how to put a sign in the parking lot—"

"The famous parking lot!" exclaimed Nour. "I've heard plenty about that from my mother."

"Nothing too bad," assured Rana.

Nour gave her a skeptical look. "You were pretty mad, Mamti." She leaned forward. "She called you some names. I'm not sure how they translate from Arabic, but they aren't polite."

"Oh, thank you, Nour," said Rana, putting a hand over her face. "That is useful."

"Just telling the truth," said Nour, grinning. "I don't want to lie to your new friend."

Marianne grinned. "Don't worry, Rana. If you ask Zeke, I'm sure he'll tell you a similar story about the things I called you."

"Hm." Rana glared at her daughter. "Zeke's behavior is not my business. Nour's is."

"I'm thirty-three! When does my behavior become my own business?"

"It's always a parent's business," said Marianne. "When you're sixty and your mother is ninety, it will still be her business how you behave."

Rana nodded approvingly.

"Oh, fine, gang up on me. And see, I'm sorry, I interrupted," said Nour, laughing. "You were talking about the parking lot."

"I was?" Marianne shook her head, smiling. "Oh, right. We've been doing research to keep anyone but customers from parking in our lot, but it as far as anyone can tell, the sale doesn't have any paperwork filed. It's making it difficult to prove we can put up a sign."

"Well," said Nour. "This is why I keep all my paperwork." She shook her head. "That sounds very frustrating."

Marianne sighed. "I've always thought of suite *B* as part of my home, even though I know the bakery is unlikely to have enough business to need both sides of the building. But it makes me sad. I used to play over there when I was a kid, back when it was storage for our stuff, before my dad sold it."

"How old were you?" asked Nour. "When the landlord's father bought it?"

"Oh, about eight," replied Marianne. "It was a long time ago."

"Fifty years, isn't it?" said Rana. "No wonder the paperwork isn't quite all in order anymore." She spooned the last piece of lamb onto a piece of naan. "I'm glad I rented here, despite all the confusion." She smiled at Marianne. "Swanley has been good to me."

"I'm glad, Mamti," said Nour. "You deserve a rest." She yawned.

"Speaking of rest, I should get you home." Rana picked up the check and slid a few bills inside, shushing Marianne's protests. "I said we were treating you, and we are."

Marianne sat back, full and sleepy. "Well, I can't argue with that. Thank you." She stood, stretching. "You'll come by before you leave to go home?" she asked Nour. "I need to repay the meal and take you both out."

Nour nodded and then pulled her into a loose hug. "It's wonderful to meet you," she said. "My Mamti likes you an awful lot. I can see why."

Marianne hugged her back and then stepped back as Rana ushered her daughter back out into the night. She followed more slowly, heading home.

Chapter Ten

Marianne sometimes just sat down on the couch and let time pass quietly for a half hour or so, decompressing from customers and sugar and butter. This had been a particularly long day, and she needed the moment to herself. She let her thoughts drift as she relaxed into the faded cushions, remembering her grandfather and father sitting together in this room fifty years earlier, joking and smiling together. She didn't know what they were laughing at—the memory didn't include that detail—but she remembered how strange she'd felt, seeing her dad laugh. She hadn't realized how much she'd noticed but not understood back then.

The doorbell sounded loudly, jerking Marianne from her thoughts. Rana had mentioned she might stop by Marianne's to watch the latest *Great British Baking Show* episode after dropping Nour at the airport, and Marianne's heart sped up a little against her will. She took a quick glance in the mirror as she passed, ensuring her hair looked somewhat presentable and she didn't have too many butter stains on the apron she hadn't managed to take off yet since closing time. She was excited to have a new friend, she told herself, ignoring the butterflies in her stomach. She knew Rana was attractive—knew she was attracted to her, knew they had the chemistry she so rarely felt with anyone and was therefore completely unequipped for when feelings did hit—but Zeke's (and Ray's, and Joe's, and Kevin's) teasing aside, she didn't need romance. And besides, it had been long enough since she last felt that way about someone that she could almost rationalize the butterflies away by calling the sensations reflux. Almost, but not quite.

She hurried down the steps and pulled open the door, a smile already spreading on her face. She'd bring out some of the leftover cheesy scones, she decided, and that bottle of wine she'd saved from last week's basket from her cheese supplier. Did Rana drink? She didn't even know. She thought Rana was Muslim, and didn't that mean no alcohol? Fatima's mother drank, but her father didn't and neither did she, and they were the only other Muslims Marianne knew. It must be one of those things that depended on the person. She would ask. Rana wouldn't be offended—

Kevin stood shivering on her doorstep in the winter wind, flecks of snow in his hair and a sheepish smile on his face. "Hi," he said as her face fell. "I take it I'm not who you were expecting?" He shifted awkwardly. "I can come back another day."

"Oh," said Marianne. "No, that's all right. Did you need something?"

"I was wondering if we could talk."

"That doesn't sound good," said Marianne. "But since we're already divorced, I can't imagine it's all that bad. Come on in." She stepped to one side, letting Kevin pass her, and shut the door after one more hopeful glance outside.

She followed Kevin up to her apartment, taking his coat and hanging it in the closet. "Want a drink?" she asked.

"When have I ever said no?" Kevin replied with a flash of white teeth. He reached in his coat pocket and pulled out a paper bag. "I bear gifts." He handed her the packet.

"Fancy olives!" Marianne's annoyance faded at the sight of the pint container inside.

"With the marinated feta from that ritzy store in Woonsocket," said Kevin. "I remember how much you liked them."

Marianne pulled a plate from the cabinet and the bottle of wine she'd been considering sharing with Rana. Now that she thought about it, she *was* pretty sure Rana didn't drink. If she did, she'd get another, better bottle to share with her. "All right, you've bribed me sufficiently. What do you want to talk about?"

Kevin sat on the couch and leaned forward as Marianne perched on the armchair across from him. He rested his elbows on his knees and nodded his thanks as Marianne set a wine glass on a coaster in front of him. "I think Luke Leventi is keeping the city from giving you information."

Marianne blinked. "Really? Why?" She shook her head. "That doesn't make any sense. The parking lot being full hurts Rana's business, which hurts his prospects of continuing to get rent from her. And I haven't found anything on that, not really." She didn't want to mention the will quite yet.

Kevin raised his eyebrows. "Rana? You're on a first name basis with your neighbor now?"

"She's nice! And it's not her fault suite *B* is such a sore spot for me."

"So, you finally buried the hatchet?"

Marianne smiled. "I'm being neighborly; that's all." She shook her head. She wasn't telling him anything more than that. It wasn't his business. "Why do you think Luke is keeping things from me?"

He sighed. "I'm not sure. It's just a feeling, I guess. But I tried to look into your last survey—I know, I know, you don't want my help, but I was curious—and the records section it's in is closed for water damage repair. And, coincidentally, so is the assessor's tax file room." He tapped the table with a finger. "And you know who's the building maintenance guy in city hall?"

"Paulie Laurence." Luke Leventi's long-time girlfriend's younger brother did side jobs for the family whenever they needed repairs on their properties. "That's a little bit of a stretch, Kevin. Don't you think? And I hope you didn't do anything but look around."

"I only looked. I promise. I didn't even take anything out. And I thought I was being paranoid, too, until three separate city employees asked why I was so interested in your property. I might be jumpy, but I'm also pretty good at knowing when there's something funny going on in local government."

"I know you are." Marianne sat back, thinking. "What's he so interested in? Why doesn't he want me to fix this?"

"I don't know, but I don't like it." He tapped his fingers again. "I told you. I have a feeling. I wanted to give you a heads' up. He's planning something. I'm sure of it now," He shook his head. "Whatever it is, I can guarantee it's not going to be good for your business. But what could it be?"

They drank the wine companionably for a few minutes, mulling over the question.

Marianne looked at Kevin. The feeling she'd had a few days earlier was intensifying, sitting with him here where they'd spent so much time. He wasn't the man she'd married, but he wasn't the one she'd divorced anymore either. She didn't love him the way she used to, but he was a part of her life, someone she trusted with everything but her heart. She'd known him fifty years and he was and would always be the father of her children. Things had solidified between them lately, his moods not bothering her the way they used to, good or bad. He knew her, and she knew him. And he knew the town better than anyone else. Maybe he could help. "Zeke and I went through some of the old records here a few nights ago. We found a will," she said, breaking the silence. "From my dad."

Kevin fumbled the olive he was stacking on a cracker, catching it before it fell to the table. "Really?"

"In the old cabinet. With the deed from Marvelle."

"The original deed?" Kevin whistled. "From the original sale back in the nineteenth century? Oh, your dad would have loved to see that. Danny loved that sort of thing. The real original?"

"That's the one." She smiled. "The paper was still in perfect shape, and I saw Marvelle Windmere's signature right on there, preserved like it was signed yesterday. You wouldn't believe it."

"And, wait, I thought your dad left you everything as his next of kin? I didn't think he had a will. Or a need for one. He only had you and the kids. Unless his brother's kids had something to do with this?"

"No, nothing like that. It's just—he didn't write a will, not as far as anyone knew. And he never filed this one anywhere, or there's no indication he did." Her smile faded. "It was dated 1969."

"Oh," said Kevin. He hadn't known them then, but he knew what that year had been like for the family; now when someone was that depressed, there were resources. In 1969, Daniel Windmere had made a will because he thought he might not be around much longer. "And he never filed it with anyone?"

"No lawyer, as far as I could tell, and it was witnessed by one of his old Army buddies. A guy who died a few years later."

"Well, it's not as if there was anyone else to dispute you for what he left," said Kevin. "So, it's all right we didn't find it then."

"I have to look at it more carefully." Marianne took a sip of her wine. "Something about the whole thing is a little strange."

"How so?"

"It didn't make sense, the way he wrote it. He didn't mention that the property had been divided, just that Simon Leventi was the conservator of my part until I reached a certain age."

"He wasn't in his right mind, Marianne. Just like my dad. Mine did some really strange stuff when he got back from Vietnam too. But Danny wanted you to have this place," said Kevin. "You know he did. And you're keeping the family legacy going here."

"I should have paid more attention." Marianne wrapped both hands around her wine glass, shoulders hunched. "When Dad was dying, I should have been here. I should have been learning the business like he wanted me to, not running around trying to get away. Then maybe I could have brought it back to what it was back when Granddad was running it."

"You didn't know," said Kevin. He leaned across the table toward her, smiling a little as he looked around the little kitchen he'd spent so much time in the year before they were married. "You needed out of here, Marianne, you know you did."

"Didn't know you'd noticed, back then."

Kevin's smile turned sheepish. "I didn't. Not then." He studied his hands. "I thought you married me because you were so in love with me. Took me till this year to realize you were running away from something, not toward me."

Marianne started, eyes widening. "Who are you and what have you done with my ex-husband?"

"Hey!" Kevin shook his head. "That's not very nice."

"Seriously, Kev, when did you get so self-aware?"

"Age, I guess," said Kevin. "Age and getting tired." He smiled. "And a little tough love from the ladies in my life."

"Well, I guess the work I put in with you was worth something after all.'

"It only took forty years." He smiled, the ghost of his old charm rearing its head. "And it wasn't all you. I did some of it myself. And all those PTA moms you like to make fun of me for loved talking about feelings."

"Always the ladies' man." She shook her head. "You really don't think I should have taken the bakery right away?"

"I don't."

"And not just because of your career?"

Kevin shook his head. "We could have had both. That's my fault as much as yours."

She smiled. "Thanks, Kevin. For saying that, and for coming here tonight." She reached out and patted his hand. "You know, the kids have been on me to see you more often." She shook her head. "I think Janie has always held out hope we might get back together, no matter how many times I tell her it's not going to happen."

Kevin winced. "I have to talk to that girl. She's stubborn."

"Like her father." Marianne grinned. "And her mother."

"She sure is."

They sat in silence for a moment; then Kevin sighed and glanced at his watch. "Hey, thank you for the drink, but I'm due at Ray's for poker night. See you tomorrow morning for coffee?"

Marianne got up, walking him to the door with a smile. "It'll be waiting for you."

*

Before she let Kevin or anyone else try to resolve things, Marianne had to take a stab at them herself. She wasn't going to let other people solve this for her. Because despite everything, Luke was her father's best friend's son, someone she'd grown up thinking of as a cousin and neighbor. If this was all a misunderstanding of some sort, if it could be resolved without any enmity or lawyers or any of that, if there was some simple explanation that would fix it, she couldn't miss that chance. It was a very small chance, and she was probably not using her best judgment trying to talk to him, but she owed that much, at least, to her father's memory.

She couldn't say she and Luke had ever been friends, or even the type of near-family that could show up unannounced at somebody's house—even when both their dads had been alive, their relationship hadn't been like that. She sometimes wondered if her father and

Luke's had a fling, sometime in the past, with the way the two of them relied on each other and danced around each other. They'd been codependent and intertwined, switching from distant to close and back again week to week. But she wasn't going to speculate on her father's sexuality. If he hadn't seen fit to reveal it while he was alive, it wasn't her business now. But it would maybe explain the trust he'd put in the other man.

Luke held what he called office hours at the Lucky Dog Pub every Monday night, ever since the campaign started, from seven to nine in the evening. She didn't want to interfere with the campaign, or get involved in any way, but she figured she could catch him on his way out the door, maybe see if he'd grab a drink or something with her while they discussed their family history.

He'd stationed himself in the back of the bar, holding court at the big table that stretched across the rear of the room with a small group of locals clustered around him. Marianne settled in on a stool to wait, ordering a beer from Carol behind the bar. Carol slid it over to her and then leaned over, tucking her long black hair behind one ear and saying, "You're not planning to pay court to his lordship over there?"

Marianne laughed. Carol didn't like Luke. She hadn't for years, ever since Luke and her sister's bad breakup back in the early eighties. He'd dumped Frances for a blonde cheerleader whose name Marianne had long since forgotten while Carol and Frances and their family were on vacation visiting their grandparents in Venezuela. Her sister Frances held no grudge, and, in fact, had campaigned for him this election, but that was big sisters for you. "Not yet," she said, taking a sip of her beer. "I'm going to try to catch him on the way out. Family business."

"Hm." Carol set a dish of peanuts down beside Marianne. "Well, it's nice to see you in here, even if it's only to visit our local celebrity." She smiled. "We haven't seen you around much lately."

"What do you mean?" Marianne shook her head. "I saw you last week. Blueberry muffins, right?"

"Seeing you working is one thing." Carol rolled her eyes. "We never see you out on the town having fun anymore. Not for years."

"Well. I'll try to come around more often," said Marianne. "But going out to bars when you're thirty and when you're almost sixty is a little different."

Carol laughed. "You're telling me, sweetie. And I know you get up early and all that. But still." She paused. "That reminds me. Nellie wanted to see if we could set up a meeting with you. Something about those new cheese crackers you were selling the other day." She grinned. "I think Nellie wants a new salty snack, one that won't bother the peanut allergy crowd."

"You'll get the gluten crowd complaining instead," warned Marianne. "But tell her to give me a call."

"Your boy is on the move," said Carol, and Marianne gulped down the last swig of her beer.

"Thanks," she said, pushing bills across the bar. "And I'll see you around, Carol."

"Yeah, yeah." Carol waved her off. "I know where to find you."

Marianne slid from the stool and hurried toward the exit as Luke extracted himself from a crowd of well-wishers and made his way through the bar. She caught him as he reached the entryway. "Luke!" she said, stepping toward him. "Can we talk a minute?"

He turned, his eyes guarded for a moment before his face broke into a genuine-looking smile. Of course, she assumed he'd been perfecting the grin the whole campaign, so she didn't take it at face value. She'd learned long ago not to do so with him. "Marianne," he said. "What can I do for you?"

"Could we grab a drink, maybe?" she asked. "I've got something I have to talk to you about."

"Sure." He slid into a booth, gesturing to the bench across from him. "I'm all ears for my future constituents. Have you finally decided to endorse me? You know a town institution like yours could do me some good."

She laughed. "We don't endorse candidates. You know that." She paused. "It's about the parking lot and suite B, actually, not the bakery. I need information on the sale."

"The sale?" His gaze was curious. "What sale is that?"

"When your dad bought suite B," she said. "I'm trying to find a survey so I can get the city to enforce a customers-only parking policy."

"That was a long time ago, Marianne. You remember how rough that time was. That might take some time to find." Something about the statement bothered Marianne, beyond the patronizing tone. He was four when his father bought the building, she recalled. He certainly didn't have a memory of it.

"I'd like to get a new survey done," she continued, "but city hall doesn't have a copy of the deed for the split on file. The only one I have is from the 1880s. If you had a copy of a recent survey, or even the deed, I would really appreciate a look."

"That's a lot to ask for a parking dispute."

"It's interfering with my business. And your tenant's business too. Could you look?"

Luke looked at his watch and sighed. "Marianne, I don't have time for this right now. I'm in the middle of a campaign. Is this really the most important issue facing the town?"

"No, but—"

"Then you can come find me after I win," he continued. "I'll look into it then." He slid out of the booth. "Nice to see you, Marianne."

As he strode out the door, Marianne stared after him. That had been quite the brush-off. She wondered what in the world he thought it was going to accomplish. She knew he didn't want to look into the situation; that was for sure. If he had a deed, he would have said so; unlike her father, and to some extent her, Luke's father and Luke himself were extremely tidy people. Her father joked once that half their realty empire was built on filing systems. He didn't want her asking about suite B. He'd have been happy to search his files if he did, happy for a chance to have her owe him a favor.

She followed him out more slowly, waving to Carol behind the bar as she went. Outside in the parking lot, Luke climbed into his BMW and pulled away.

Marianne sent a silent apology to her father, who, despite being a veteran, had avoided conflict his whole life and desperately tried to make peace between the people he cared about. *Sorry, Dad. I think this fight with Simon's kid is going to be more trouble than I bargained for when I started looking into the parking lot.*

The walk back to Windmere Bakery took her down the busiest strip of Main Street, and she took the time slowly. The night was nicer than she'd expected, a mild wind blowing through the bare trees in the park across the street, and the streetlights cast a warm glow over the cobblestone sidewalks. They'd been redone a few years ago, restored to their turn of the century glory, and in the dark with the imitation gas lamps, she could have been walking along her grandfather's Main Street. The breeze sent goose bumps down the nape of her neck and she pulled her coat closer around her.

Ahead, the bakery in the distance looked exactly as it had for a hundred years, white-washed brick with narrow windows on the second floor and the Windmere Bakery sign in gold lettering sparkling in the light of the lamp that stuck out from the building just above it.

None of this was good.

Chapter Eleven

Luke Leventi's ads were everywhere, and they grated on Marianne even more after her encounter with him Monday night.

She glared at the bus-stop bench a few days later as she sat at the red light at the corner of Tremont and Oak, wondering why a guy who controlled so much in town already felt the need to run for office and get even more wrapped up in the community for what seemed like little payoff. Maybe he was considering a run for president someday? Why else would he be wasting so much time and money on this campaign with all its ads and interviews? And where was he getting that money? He was wealthy, yes, but not wealthy enough to be buying market-wide airtime and this much physical advertising. Marianne had looked into advertising a few times for the bakery and each time had concluded word of mouth was much cheaper and much more effective. Besides, all the ads were by various PACs. What kind of candidate for a house primary had this many PACs? It didn't make sense.

The light changed and she took the left onto Tremont and then the right onto Chestnut, pulling into the Wilshire Market Basket parking lot and into a spot just past the entrance. She needed something besides falafel and croissants in her apartment; there was only so much restaurant food she could eat before she needed to make herself a couple days' worth of salads.

Someone called her name as she stepped up on the curb, and she turned to see Michael Blake. He looked friendlier out of his police uniform and pushing a stroller. She waved as he wheeled over, dodging a festive broccoli display.

"This is Brady Nicole Blake," said Michael. "Brady, this is Marianne. Her coffee is the thing your mom missed most while she was pregnant."

"How old is she?" asked Marianne, smiling down at the tiny face gazing up at her. "She's beautiful."

"Five weeks," said Michael proudly. "This is her first trip to the grocery store. We need some diapers, and Mom needs some alone time. Doesn't she, sweetie?"

"I remember those days." Marianne reached out and stroked a finger along a tiny closed fist poking out from the blankets. "I hope you're giving Sally all the help she asks for."

Michael gave a very tired laugh. "Doing my best, Ms. Windmere. But you know how it is at the station."

"They don't give you any leave? She's your baby, too, you know."

"Oh, I know." He grinned. "Everybody says she's got my eyes already. But I only get two weeks, which I guess is better than most towns, so the Chief said I shouldn't complain. I've been stretching them out best I can, couple days a week, but I finally ran out."

He pushed the carriage around the lettuce and Marianne followed, nodding sympathetically.

"And you know how busy we get when the winter starts hitting," he continued. "This is my one day off this week. The rest of it's been spent dealing with people ready to murder their neighbors over parking space savers. I had to take somebody in on Tuesday for assault by lawn chair. And not to mention security at the election events—" He shook his head, grabbing a couple cans of beans from a shelf as Marianne played peekaboo with Brady, who hiccupped and drooled. "It's going to be a busy winter."

"Sorry for adding to your load," said Marianne. "You can imagine the complaints I get about that lot though."

"Oh, I know. They call us about it too. And it's not going to get any better once the new coffee shop goes in."

Marianne froze. "New coffee shop? What are you talking about?"

"The Dunkin'?" He looked up, confused, then his face fell. "I mean, no, nothing. I'm tired. I must have been confusing your parking lot with someone else's."

"What Dunkin', Mickey?"

He half-smiled at the old nickname, but his eyes stayed worried. "Ms. Windmere—" He looked down at his baby, who shook her fists jerkily, barely missing punching herself in the face. His face softened. "I don't know anything, okay? I shouldn't tell you anything. It's just that the Dunkin' brass have been around town lately, meeting with Mr. Leventi and the folks from that startup. You know he's campaigning on that whole 'bring the city to Swanley' nonsense. I guess this is the start." He looked up. "Didn't Kevin tell you? He filed all the permits with the City Council."

"Kevin's retired, remember?"

His face fell even further. "Right. I forgot. He wouldn't know anymore." He turned his eyes to Marianne's, pleadingly. "Please forget I said anything. I don't think the chief would like me spreading Mr. Leventi's business around, especially since they're family. I'm exhausted; that's all."

Marianne patted his arm consolingly. "This is why you guys need more family leave. I won't say anything to the chief. I promise."

Michael looked somewhat reassured, though his eyes had that wild look of sleep-deprived panic she recalled from her own three children's babyhoods. *They have to start giving these guys more paternity leave. I don't want a guy with this little sleep running around with a gun. Michael's always been a nice kid, but no sleep combined with power and weapons is a recipe for disaster, especially in a town getting bigger and more complex by the day as Boston prices skyrocketed and folks moved west.*

"Give me a call sometime," she said. "I'll watch Brady for a few hours while the bakery's closed. Let you two get some sleep."

He brightened. "Really?"

She nodded. "You watched my kid. I can watch yours." She grinned. "I won't even charge your exorbitant rates. Ten dollars an hour was pretty high back then, Mickey."

"Hey, that was for my CPR certification!" Laughing, Michael nodded. "I'll take you up on that. Thanks, Ms. Windmere."

"Anytime, Mickey. You be good, all right?" She missed having babies around. And it wouldn't hurt to have a cop in her debt either.

His cocky grin reminded her too much of Kevin at that age. "I always am."

She waved him off as he headed toward the baby aisle, and she broke off back toward the produce.

A Dunkin' Donuts? In Swanley?

Swanley had always been one of those odd towns that resisted chains. They didn't have a Starbucks—the nearest one was over in Wilshire, and Marianne's kids, when they were home, sometimes snuck her frappuccinos when the weather got too hot. And across the border in Milford sat a McDonald's and a Chili's, but when TGI Fridays had tried to open a location out in the old Swanley industrial area, there'd been a near-revolt. Would things be different now? That had been twenty years earlier, and most of the strongest resisters had died or moved away, replaced by young transplants from the city. Some of them might miss the convenience of Dunkin'. And the new blood had been largely a good thing for the town, diversifying a mostly white, mostly American-born town into something a little closer to the rest of the country. This wasn't gentrification, as much as she'd like to call it that. This was growth. But had her business grown with the town, or was she stuck in the past like some of her grouchier neighbors? Was the bakery going to be left behind for coffee shops with apps and corporations behind them?

Marianne had always had a preference for locally owned stores, especially given her own bakery's history, but she didn't necessarily have a problem with chains as long as they treated their communities and their workers well. A donut and coffee shop right next to hers, though, with the low prices that a huge chain like Dunkin' could afford to sell at would not bode well for her business.

Maybe it was only a rumor, she mused as she loaded her cart with eggs and butter. Maybe it was Mickey's sleep deprivation-addled brain confusing things. Maybe she was catastrophizing. But then she remembered those men Rana had seen lurking around her shop, and the look on Luke Leventi's face when he'd stopped by a few weeks earlier. It had been covetous, and it had been plotting. Replacing Rana's store with a Dunkin' Donuts would drive Marianne out of business, and he knew the building wouldn't sell for as much as she'd need it to in order to buy a house. He'd offer her something far below the bakery's value now, once he killed her business.

How had her father gotten mixed up with that family? Why had he let them into their life? She knew he and Simon had grown up together, that their fathers and grandfathers had fought together, but still, hadn't he had any inkling of what might happen?

Chapter Twelve

All of this was speculation, and in all of it, Marianne had forgotten a very important thing.

She had a witness to the deal, if she was lucky.

The morning rush had faded away, and Joe sat in his usual chair, drinking his coffee and reading the paper, and Marianne finished helping the last customer in line before squeezing out from behind the counter and bringing him a Danish. He looked up and smiled at her. "Hi, honey. What're you trying to bribe out of me with this lovely confection?"

Marianne laughed. "No bribe. Just wanted to ask you about a little of our history here."

He smiled, his dentures very white against his creased dark skin. "Well, you know I always want to talk history. That's the job of old folks, you know. The future's for the young, like you and Ezekiel."

"I'm fifty-eight, Joe; you know that. Hardly young."

"When you're staring down the barrel of a century in a couple years, fifty-eight is plenty young. Now, as you've so gently reminded me, my time on Earth is not eternal. What did you want to talk about?"

"Can you tell me about Simon Leventi and my dad? What made my dad turn half the building over to him?"

Joe smiled and leaned back in his chair, fingers running over the old wood of the table before him. "Well, that was a while ago, but yes, I remember. Couldn't forget it if I tried."

"Didn't he know better than to do business with the Leventis?"

"Hah! At that time, they weren't *the Leventis*, not as you know them." He shook his head. "No, there was just Elias Leventi and his son, Simon, and they were your father's neighbors growing up."

"So, they didn't have money back then?"

"Nobody had money back then, honey. Not in this town. Back then, we had the factory, and everybody worked there. If they were white, they might someday be a foreman or a manager. Everybody else just wanted to get by."

"So, how'd they get it? The wealth—the power—I mean. How'd they come to own half the town?"

"Well, your daddy helped," Joe sighed. "You're bringing up a lot of old nonsense; you know that? All of this is in the past. Nothing to be done about it now."

"It's already up, Joe. I got a call from the town that they're going to be doing an audit on my property. And the health inspector showed up. All within a week of me asking to see the records on the building."

"You've always known how to stir up trouble. You're like your great-grandpa that way."

"I am?"

Joe tapped the table with gnarled brown fingers. "He always used to say he started the business with one pocketful of luck and another of dust. He had a way with words, your granddad's daddy, Marvelle. The dust, he used to say, was all his family had left after the war and also what got kicked up when he started building his bakery in this one-horse town. People didn't like it, see, because he hired whoever he wanted—gender, color, religion be damned. He wanted people who could work."

He grinned. "People didn't like that, not in this old Puritan town. But he didn't care one bit."

"I didn't know that," said Marianne. "He was a good man?"

"Oh, he had his flaws, for sure," said Joe. "His wife would've told you all of them. So would his mistresses. But yes, he was better than most." He leaned back in his chair. "I'll try to tell you what I remember about the two of them, best I can. That's all I can offer, Marianne. It was a long time ago, and the place was different then."

"So, tell me about it."

"You know Luke Leventi, of course, who owns half the town these days. And his father, Simon."

"Of course, I do."

"Well, Simon had a girlfriend back in the fifties. Said he was going to marry her too. Josie Barnes, her name was."

"Why have I never heard of her? Why didn't they get married? This must have been before Luke's mom."

"You've never heard of her because she died, Marianne." Joe shook his head. "Tragic thing it was, too, her dying like that."

Joe was really getting into storytelling mode now, the gleam in his eye driving out the caution of earlier. Marianne hoped she didn't get any customers for a few minutes, because Joe was a man who needed to stretch out a good dramatic story as long as it took. "Like what?"

"In the accident." He leaned forward, pointing a finger at Marianne. "Your father was there. So was the old mayor."

"Mayor Bryce? He was there?" Bill Bryce had been mayor of Swanley most of Marianne's life. She remembered him as a big, distant figure, looming large over city events. He still was, from his stately home on the north side of town. No one saw much of him, but he wrote steaming letters to the local papers and huge checks to his favored candidates for local and state elections. He had to be coming up on ninety now, a few years older than her dad would have been had he lived longer. Nearly Joe's age.

"Oh, yes, he and your father and Simon were great friends back then."

"That can't be right." Marianne's father had hated the old mayor, had voted against him at every election, and cursed him every time something went wrong in the town even if there was no way the problem was his fault.

"Just telling you what I know," said Joe. "They were thick as thieves, those three, and Josie too. She and your father were the best of friends. People always wondered if your father had more than a friendly fondness for her."

"This was before my mom, right?"

"Oh, yes. Your mother was the foreigner in town."

"Foreigner? She was born in Worcester."

Joe laughed. "Her parents weren't born in America. That meant foreigner back then. By the time she got to Swanley in the last few years of high school, the groups were already cemented. You have to understand, in those times all those kids had been together since kindergarten. Bill Bryce and your daddy and Simon Leventi played baseball together in the lot behind the old schoolhouse while their fathers were away working on the railroads after the war, helping the country rebuild itself."

"I know he and Simon were friends. But I didn't know the mayor was part of their group."

"He was the ringleader. And he was driving the night Josie died."

"He killed a girl, and they still elected him?"

"Well, there was no proof he was the one driving, you see? And his granddad was the mayor too. He and Josie were thrown from the car when it hit the Creeley farm's stone wall. That was back in, oh, '54, I believe." He shook his head. "Simon took it hard. Your daddy did too. And things weren't the same with Bill and them after that. Those two stuck together, and Bill started running with the North Swanley crowd, getting ready to run things like his family wanted. Simon and Bill eventually reconciled enough to do business, but your dad and him never did."

"So what happened then? I mean, how did Simon get so much land in town if he was on Bill's bad side?"

Joe swirled the coffee in the base of his mug. "The next few years, Mr. Leventi—Elias, that is—started getting plenty of contracts with the city—he was a builder, you see, putting up all the new town buildings in the sixties." He shook his head. "I think Daniel—your old man—and Simon put some kind of pressure on Bill."

"Like blackmail? No, not my dad."

"Your father might've gotten cold feet, at some point; I don't know. And then he signed up and headed off to Asia, to the war, even though he was too old for the draft. He wanted to help his country, but he came back changed. He didn't have the stomach for business anymore, I believe. All I know is Leventi's fortunes kept rising, and so did Bill Bryce's. I don't know if Simon ever forgave him for the death of his girlfriend, but he most definitely became a very wealthy man at the hands of Mayor Bryce."

"And all this made them closer. My dad and Simon, that is."

"I'd say so. That's why he trusted Simon with the business while he was away."

"And why he let him have suite B."

"That's likely too." Joe shook his head. "I wasn't around for that deal; I'm sorry to say. That's the year my mother took a turn for the worse. I wasn't there for your dad at the end, and I'll always be sorry for that. But when I got back, Simon had the place running smooth. I loved your daddy, but he didn't have much business sense. Of course, he did have plenty on his plate at that time. Lord knows what he was thinking when he passed over the keys. All I can say is that the two of them argued plenty, but Danny always let Simon have his way in the end."

"Joe, you know everything about this town. I'll never stop being astonished."

Joe laughed. "Well, it's not a big town, honey. You of all people know that. And I was working for your granddaddy at the time. And nobody thought I'd be listening when they had all their big emotional chats. I wasn't paid much more attention than the broom I pushed or the bike I rode." He smiled. "Your family's been good to me, but this town took a long time to change."

"I'm sorry," said Marianne, not sure what she could say to that. She had had her issues with the town, sure, but Joe had seen so much, been through so much, in nearly a century in Swanley. He'd seen the town go from horse and buggy to electric cars, from telegraph to smartphones, and he'd been there through it all. His father had fought in World War I, his grandfather in the Civil War, and he had marched in the '60s alongside heroes. And now he sat in her bakery most mornings, enjoying rest and the company of his great-grandson, who was fighting his own battle for rights. Marianne needed to comp the guy more coffees.

"What do you think I should do?" she asked. "If my dad sold the building, if Leventi owns it, how can I keep him from doing what he's planning to do? I can't have a Dunkin' Donuts in my great-grandfather's building. I can't, Joe. "

"Oh, old Marvelle wouldn't like that one bit, my dear. Not one bit. He could rail against the wealthy with the best of them, that man."

"So, what can I do?"

Joe laughed, a low, creaking sound. "Do? Marianne, that family does what they want around here these days. You've never gone up against them, not really. All most of us can do is get out of their way, most times."

"He's going to replace me with a *Dunkin' Donuts*. Windmere Bakery has been in Swanley for a century and a half, Joe! And he's going to replace me with a place that sells Celtics donuts! And then once he drives me out of business, he's going to knock my bakery down and build a drive-through or something!"

"Nothing wrong with the Celtics, Marianne. Not when they're winning like they are now." Joe sighed. "If you're going to fight this, dear, you're going to need to get ready for him to fight dirty. He's got a lot to lose, you know, with the race coming up."

"I've got my whole livelihood to lose, Joe. He's the one who's got to watch out for me."

Chapter Thirteen

Marianne had a mission now, and she wasn't going to let anything get in her way. As soon as she handed the bakery over to Zeke for the slow last couple of hours of the afternoon, she hurried back to the newly cleaned filing cabinet. Deed in hand, carefully slipped into a page protector and tucked into a folder, Marianne marched right down to city hall.

As she neared the building, a familiar figure, coming down the steps from the front door, caught her eye. It took Marianne a moment to recognize Doris Chanthavongsa, her brightly patterned blouse and dark jeans a sharp contrast to her usual postal blues. As the door to city hall swung closed behind her, Marianne called out across the street. "Doris!"

Doris looked up and smiled. She looked tired, dark shadows under her eyes and a slump in her shoulders Marianne hadn't seen there before.

"Is everything all right?" asked Marianne as she crossed the street to the city hall side.

"I'm not sure," said Doris, and then she looked up, her face clearing. "Oh, Marianne, hi. I didn't see you there."

"What's going on?"

Doris shook her head. "Just voting. I'm going to be out of town on election day. I wanted to make sure I got everything settled before I went."

"Where are you going?" Marianne smiled. "Not that it's any of my business, sorry. I know you're not working."

"No, that's all right." Doris turned her tired smile toward Marianne. "I'm trying to help with a family problem; that's all."

"Anything I can help you with?"

Doris laughed. "Oh, no, thank you."

Marianne nodded, wanting to press because Doris looked upset but not wanting to overstep the boundary they'd always worked within. They'd known each other fifteen years, but they'd been each other's customers that whole time. Doris's private life wasn't any of her business. She'd like to think of Doris as a friend, but she wasn't quite sure if she could; they never saw each other outside their professional capacities, after all, and Doris didn't visit out of wanting to—she was legally required to stop by Marianne's shop every day, and there was always the possibility that she was just trying to maintain a cordial relationship with someone she wouldn't want to see otherwise. "Well, I hope things work out," she said. "And let me know if you need anything."

Doris smiled, a little more honestly this time. "Thanks, Marianne. I will. See you tomorrow." And with that, she turned and headed toward the parking lot. Marianne watched her go, frowning and then climbed the steps and pulled open the heavy oak door of the Swanley City Hall.

The sign for the records hall had a small sign warning that it was under maintenance, but she didn't let that dissuade her. She made her way up to the second floor and followed the corridor down to the end, where a round older white woman sat reading a thick novel with a spaceship on the cover.

"Hi," said Marianne. "Sorry to bother you. I need to see a copy of my property survey."

The woman looked up, sliding an index card into the paperback and setting it to one side.

"It's no bother. It's what they pay me to do. What's the property?" she asked, sliding a pair of glasses onto her snub nose. She clicked her mouse, the ancient desktop whirring to life. "And what company conducted the survey?"

"It's 121 Main Street, and—well, I don't know who did it."

"What year?"

"Well, we sold part of the property in the sixties, so there must have been a survey then. In 1968?"

The woman pulled the glasses back off, setting them aside and turning in her chair. "So you don't know if there was one?"

"If we split the lot, there would have to be, wouldn't there?"

"There should be." The woman cocked her head. "Hmm, 121 Main. That's the bakery, isn't it?"

"That's right."

The woman smiled. "My husband loves the muffins there—he's always bringing them to his office. And we've fallen in love with the new place next door." She put her glasses back on. "Well. Let me take a look." She typed a few keywords into the program she had open and then hit enter. "We've been planning to stop by for pies this year before Easter—will you be doing the preorders again this year?"

"Of course," Marianne answered. "We're trying a new pie this year, too, a fruits-of-the-forest theme. Come by sometime, and I'll put you on the early-bird list."

She grinned, delighted, and held out a pale, wide hand. "I'm Jolene. Jolene McGonnegal. I've seen you around, but I don't think we've ever met in person."

Marianne shook her hand. "Marianne Windmere."

"Windmere. Of course. You said it was your family's." The computer pinged, and Jolene looked back at the screen and then frowned. "Well, that's odd," she said.

"What's odd?" asked Marianne.

"There's no survey record in 1968. Let me try expanding the parameters." She changed some fields. "I'll try 1965-1975, in case it was entered late."

"I might have the date off by a year or two," admitted Marianne. "I wasn't exactly running the business back then."

Jolene smiled. "No, I'd imagine not." The computer pinged again.

"Still nothing?" guessed Marianne as Jolene's frown deepened.

"No," replied Jolene. She widened the parameters again. "Let's try 1960 through 1980." Her face brightened. "There we go. 1964. No wonder we couldn't find it!"

"That can't be right," said Marianne. "Nineteen sixty-four was before my dad even went to Vietnam. He didn't sell until he got back."

"Well, honey, that's what the system says." She looked up. "Would you like a copy of that record, at least?"

"That would probably be a good thing to have on record. What would it mean that he had a survey done? I mean, if it wasn't for a sale."

Jolene leaned back in her seat, looking up at Marianne. "Well, if he had thought about selling the property, or about applying for it to be rezoned, he might get one," she said thoughtfully. "The building had been in your family a long time, hadn't it?"

"Since 1886," said Marianne.

"So maybe he wanted to get a new deed made," said Jolene. "Many of the old ones are not exactly precise by modern standards."

"But there's nothing from the sale? And there would have to be, wouldn't there?"

Jolene nodded. "To determine where the borders were between the lots, yes, of course." She rubbed her chin. "The only other place that would be is in the deed of sale. If it's well-defined there, sometimes back then the survey wouldn't be filed, just kept in the personal possession of the two entities involved."

"Well, my dad didn't keep a copy, if he ever got one," said Marianne.

"What about the person he sold the property to?"

Marianne winced. "We're not on great terms, which is actually why I needed the survey."

"Ah." She typed some more, frowning. "I'm not seeing the sale record here," she said apologetically. "It's possible the record was lost in the fire in '76."

"So, what would that mean?" She pulled her copy of her deed out of her bag, "I have my original deed. Does that help?"

"Not unless you have the updated deed," said Jolene. "Or he does."

"So, the city has no record of the sale. That's what you're saying, right?"

Jolene grimaced. "I'm sorry, Ms. Windmere, but it looks like that's true. Either the paperwork was lost in the fire or the flood in '92, never filed, or never sold."

"Never sold?" Marianne stared at Jolene. "That— Huh. I hadn't thought of that."

"I have no idea if that's a possibility," Jolene hurried to say. "But it's one you should consider, in the full spectrum of possibilities." She shrugged. "It's much more likely the paperwork is lost." She shuffled a pile of papers on her desk to one side. "Although I have to tell you, if the city has no record of his deed filed, you're the owner on record."

"I am?"

"If there's no record, then possibly, yes." She raised a warning finger. "Possibly. Of course, there's no reason the deed wouldn't be found later, misfiled. And then where would you be?"

Marianne winced. "That's a good point. So, what can I do? I need to figure out where my property ends."

She sighed. "Unfortunately, you may have to go to court to determine the boundary if there is one. I'm not sure what that process would look like."

"Hm." Marianne wasn't sure what to do with that information. She didn't like the ambiguity of the response, that was for certain. If Luke's family had bought the property, she wanted proof. If he didn't, how had he been operating it for so long? How had no one noticed?

With that thought came a very uncomfortable realization. She'd assumed so much that might not turn out to be true when she took the bakery over. When Luke's father Simon handed Windmere Bakery's reins back to her after running it in trust for the decade after her father died—the decade when she had thought she'd rebel against the family business, and go do something else, and the decade where she'd realized the place she wanted to escape was actually exactly where she belonged—she should have gotten documents from him. She should have made sure she knew where his family ended and hers began. But she'd trusted that her father's best friend had her best interests in mind. She'd only realized otherwise in slow jolts over the next decade, as Simon stepped back from the realty empire he'd built and his less subtle, more ambitious son had stepped in.

Her business was at risk because her father had trusted his friend and his friend's family to be honest, good neighbors. And now Marianne didn't know what to think. If Simon didn't file the paperwork with city hall— and she couldn't imagine that having happened, because no one built a real estate empire like his without being very good at paperwork—where could the records be? And why hadn't her father ever confirmed everything was all set?

Her father hadn't been the most organized person in the world, Marianne knew. She had learned that quickly when she'd first started helping with the financial issues after her mother had passed away. But the big stuff didn't start to slip until near the end, long after she'd moved out and pulled away from the business and her father.

But something *had* fallen through the cracks, and now they were all dealing with the fallout—her and Zeke and Rana most of all. That was the other thing that bothered her: that Rana was suffering for her lack of research and care in the nineties. Rana, who made incredible food and kept her family afloat through so much hardship after her husband died; Rana, who'd brought some light back into Marianne's life that she hadn't even known she was missing. Rana, who might lose her livelihood and the shop she loved because of Marianne's meddling.

Marianne was suddenly glad it was Friday, the day Rana closed the Cairo Grill early to attend services at the mosque in Framingham with Fatima and her family. This was something Marianne had to work through on her own before she could include anyone else.

She thanked Jolene, zipping her coat back up and starting toward the stairs. She had so much to figure out now. So many new avenues she had to search, and no idea where to start. But she had to do something; that much she knew. She had to get clarity, and if she could get back the part of her building she'd mourned losing for the last thirty years and screw over Luke Leventi in the process? She'd take it.

Chapter Fourteen

Marianne tossed and turned most of the night, possibilities running through her head. What if they never found out what really happened? What if she confronted Luke on the issue of ownership and he took his anger out on Rana, and on Marianne's own business? He had enough connections in the town, as well as owning many of the local businesses, and he could do plenty to damage both of their reputations and customer bases.

And what if she found out her father hadn't sold the building, that it had all been a vicious misunderstanding? She didn't know if she could stand that.

She finally got out of bed around four a.m., despite it being her usual day to sleep in until six, and headed downstairs to throw some croissants and muffins in the oven for the early risers. By the time she needed to open the front door, she'd prepped the next day's pastries as well. She'd mixed batters and doughs and a huge tub of chocolate buttercream, and even made a gallon of raspberry jam. That last part was an indulgence in the decidedly not-raspberry season of December, but she'd been craving raspberry croissants. She took her time stocking the display case and grinding the beans for the coffee, pouring herself a huge mug of sweet, milky espresso. She'd usually drink it darker and more bitter, but with no one there to judge her on a cold, sleepy day, she could indulge.

The sleet kept the customers away when she opened at her usual 7:00 a.m., and since it was Zeke's day off, Kevin was the first person to walk into Windmere Bakery when he showed up around eight.

"Coffee," he said, heading straight for the register.

"Wipe your feet," she retorted, pointing at his wet footprints.

Kevin grumbled and did an about-face, scraping his shoes on the welcome mat. "Now can I have coffee?"

Marianne laughed and handed him a mug. "You sticking around today, or are you racing off to the city again? I wouldn't mind the company if you wanted to hang around."

"Slow day today," he admitted. "Suddenly I'm finding I need to rest a whole day about once a week, like some kind of Old Testament God. Isn't age grand?"

Marianne nodded sympathetically. "I'm definitely feeling it, too, in this weather." She shook her head. "Remember when we used to go hiking miles and miles every weekend? I used to know the Blue Hills trails better than parts of Swanley."

"I forgot about that." He smiled fondly. "You should retire, Marianne. We could do some of those hikes again, a little slower."

"I can't retire," Marianne replied. "What would happen to the bakery?"

He sighed. "I can't believe none of the kids are interested."

"I can," said Marianne. "They watched me give it everything and still struggle. And they've all got degrees and careers—even Jacob has a plan, now that he's finally committing to school."

"You think he's going to buckle down and finish his degree?"

"I hope so." Marianne leaned on the counter, stretching her back. It was stiff from her evening scrubbing out the ovens. "Even if he doesn't, there's nothing wrong with working for the Post Office the rest of his career. At least he'll get a pension someday. Look at Doris. She's been carrying mail twenty years, and she doesn't look a day over thirty."

"I always hoped Anna would take over," admitted Kevin. "She was the only one of our three I could see staying in Swanley."

Marianne sat down heavily on her stool. "I don't know what's going to happen to this place, Kevin. Not with everything going on."

"What do you mean?"

Marianne sighed. "There's some strange questions right now about the property; that's all. The fact that we can't find the record of who owns what part is very frustrating. And I heard a rumor Leventi wants to sell the other suite. And with the will we found, I don't know what to think. Or what to do."

"Sell it? Why would he do that?"

"Apparently, he has an offer from Dunkin' Donuts. Think about what that would do to business here."

He winced. "It wouldn't be good. I'd heard a rumor about something like that, but I didn't know it was him. And I didn't know he was planning to put it in the Cairo Grill. I should have mentioned it."

Marianne shook her head. "No reason you would have known it was relevant to me. That's all right. But it won't be good to my revenue. And it wouldn't help the parking lot issue either. What if he puts in a drive-through?"

"So, what *are* you thinking? Because I know you, Marianne, and you've got your plotting face on."

She straightened, putting her hands on her hips. "I think... I think my dad's will is the clue we need to figure this out. I think maybe he never sold it, Kevin."

"What?"

"That's the only thing that makes sense. He never sold the building, not to Simon, not to Luke, not to anybody. He asked Simon to run things over there, and then Simon slowly took it over until everyone believed he owned it. Why would my dad have ever sold it? You know what this place meant to him, especially after Grandpa died."

"There's no way." Kevin shook his head. "That's too unbelievable. How would he convince everyone?"

"Easy. He was running the place, and nobody had seen my dad up and about for months. My mom was getting sicker every day, and he was dealing with untreated PTSD. It would be simple to make people believe my family sold it to pay for Mom's treatment. And I was too young to know what was going on. By the time I took over, he could have fooled us all." The more she thought about it, the more she believed it. "But how can I prove it?"

"You have your deed, right?"

"Well, yes, but it's from 1866."

"Still, doesn't that prove you own it? Real estate law was never my specialty, but that seems right to me." He tapped the edge of the table first with his thumb and then his middle finger in a rhythm that had driven Marianne nuts when they were married.

It didn't bother her nearly as much now, and she once again sent a prayer of gratitude that they'd managed to stay friends after the divorce. They were better that way. She sighed. "I have no idea whether it's valid after all these years."

"Well, it should be filed at city hall."

"They wouldn't let me look, remember?"

"They wouldn't let *you* look; that's right." He stood, drawing himself to his full height and gave her that winning white smile he'd used in every city council campaign flyer for decades. "They'll let me in."

Marianne shifted her weight, trying to explain. "I don't want to go around the process, Kevin. The system is there for a reason."

"They're the ones who are wrong here!" Kevin shook his head, running a hand through his hair and mussing his neatly brushed silver waves loose. "I know you disapprove of how I work. That's not news to me. But sometimes the back way in works as well as—or better than—hitting from the front! If I have a key, why not let me use it?"

"Because that's cheating!" She wasn't sure how to explain it more clearly. She wasn't someone who used her connections to get what she wanted.

Kevin threw his hands up, nearly shouting, "So's taking a left on Oak Street after seven in the morning to cut your travel time by three minutes, and I've seen you do that a hundred times! This is just as close to legal!"

Marianne stared at him for a second, suddenly fighting a smile. Kevin met her eyes, his sparkling with annoyance, and then they were both laughing, the tension broken. "Jesus," said Marianne. "We've still got the fighting part of the marriage down."

"That's the only part we were ever really good at," said Kevin.

"And raising kids," corrected Marianne. "We brought up three pretty great ones."

He nodded. "That, too," he sighed. "I want to help. I love this place, despite everything. It's where our kids grew up. It's where *we* grew up. And it's good for the town. You always said the town was my favorite mistress, and you weren't exactly wrong. You know how much I love it. I don't want a Dunkin' instead of Windmere. You know I don't. So let me help you."

"Fine."

Kevin blinked, taken aback. "Really?"

She shrugged. "Yeah. Go ahead. Give it a try. I could use the help, I guess."

He stared at her. "I—all right. I will." He cleared his throat. "Well, the first step is to get that will filed with the probate court. It counts for squat until then."

"Will you help me do that?"

"I can't be your lawyer, Marianne. You know that, right? We're family, and we have a history."

"Do I need a lawyer for this?"

He shook his head. "For filing a will in probate? No, I can help you with the paperwork for that. But if things get sticky or if they aren't as easy as we're hoping they'll be, then yes, you'll need one." He smiled. "And actually, I know just the lawyer for you. If it comes to that."

"Let's do it then. Let's file it."

*

Rana's shop always smelled so good: warm and spicy and delicious. It was a nice change from the sweet floury scent of the bakery. Marianne checked out the woman she'd just handed a falafel wrap to and then snuck a bite of pickled turnip from the condiments. She didn't exactly like the flavor, but she couldn't stop eating the little pink slivers.

Rana's shop was also a break from the constant caroling and bright lights strung around town. Marianne had never been a big Christmas fan. She and Kevin had always defaulted to his Jewish traditions—despite the last name McNamara, his family had been somewhat observant of his mother's faith. She'd strung up lights along the windows in the bakery and put out snowmen cookies in the last week, filling dozens of orders for cookies for Santa. She'd never liked the Santa myth, and she especially didn't like the number of parents who requested Santa-shaped cookies to leave for him. If Santa were real, Marianne couldn't imagine him enjoying eating himself in effigy. Rana's shop was a haven for agnostic grinches like her; snowflakes in the windows cut out by her smallest customers while waiting for their food were her only sign of the season.

The door creaked open, Doris struggled through with her hands full of parcels and mail, and Marianne hurried out from behind the counter to hold the door open for her. Doris smiled and dug in her satchel, handing Marianne a few letters and a small manila envelope. "I thought I might find you here," she said. I tried to make it before you closed, but we had a couple sick calls today on top of the Christmas volume and we're all pulling double duty. Is Rana around?"

"She had to run to the back for something," said Marianne. "I'm watching the store for a minute. Do you want me to take her mail for her?"

Doris smiled gratefully. "I'm way behind. You know what this season is like." She pulled out a stack of small white envelopes and a large manila one with a barcode. "Can you sign for this one?"

Marianne took the pen and signed the scanner and then took the pile.

"Thanks, Marianne. See you tomorrow." She waved and hurried back out to her truck.

"Hope things get better out there," Marianne called after her retreating back.

"Was that Doris?" asked Rana as she reappeared from the office. "I meant to give her some mail to send out."

"Sorry," said Marianne. "She was in a rush." She offered Rana her mail. "She deputized me to deliver this."

Rana took the pile. "I think that might be a federal crime."

Marianne shrugged. "I'm a rebel. Anything good?"

Rana frowned at an envelope.

"What?"

"It's from Luke Leventi," she said, tone wary. "I've already paid my rent, and he cashed the check. What else could he want?"

"Maybe he's finally fixing that pipe in the bathroom," mused Marianne.

"I think he would call for something like that." Rana carefully tore open the envelope and pulled out the single page inside, scanning it. "This doesn't make sense."

"What doesn't?"

"This letter. It says he won't be renewing my lease."

"When does it end?"

Rana shook her head. "February. But I already called to let him know I want to stay!"

"Has he sent you a new lease?"

"No," said Rana. "He can do this?" She read the letter again, quickly. "He can do this, can't he? Because he's the landlord, he can decide I have to leave. But why? I'm paying my rent and keeping the place clean. How can he do this?"

Marianne leaned over her shoulder, scanning the letter quickly. "Oh, that ass."

"What?"

"She pointed to a paragraph near the bottom. "It says if you don't notify him with 90 days' notice by certified mail, he doesn't have to renew."

"But this lease is supposed to be renewable! When I rented the space, I told him I planned to be here at least five years! How could he not tell me he was kicking me out? That's not fair!"

"Yeah, but the lease says he can do this, unfortunately."

"I know he wants to sell the place, but he shouldn't be able to kick me out!"

"I think it's a message," said Marianne. "I think it's a message to me."

"To you?" Rana stared at her. "I'm being evicted, and you think it's about you?"

"I'm looking into his business—"

"I know you are! But this is my *life*, Marianne! You own your bakery. I don't. And now I have two months to find somewhere new." She shook her head and squeezed back behind the counter. "I don't think this is a great time for you to be here right now. Thanks for watching the shop."

"I'm sorry," Marianne offered. "I know this isn't about me. If you don't want me around, I understand." The pit of her stomach sat sour.

Rana sighed. "Just give me a little while to figure out my next steps, Marianne. I'm not ending our friendship. I need some time, all right? This is going to be awful, and you aren't making it any better."

Marianne stared at her for a moment and then turned and went back outside. She hadn't thought about what would happen if Luke found out she was investigating his claim to the building. She probably should have. She'd thought if she could prove her ownership, everything would stay the same. Except even if she did prove it, things would change. She'd be Rana's landlord. That would change everything by itself. The wild little dream she'd been holding onto of Rana growing old with her in shops side by side, partners in business and in love, fizzled and popped.

She took a deep breath. She couldn't back off now—that would ensure she never got her rightful property back. And now she'd cost Rana her security, and maybe her business, if this didn't go well. She had to figure out how to stop that sale and fix this somehow.

Chapter Fifteen

Unfortunately, nothing involving the town was going to be fast or easy, not in late December and right before the special election primary. Marianne didn't know how the week before Christmas had snuck up on her so quickly—it had been mid-November last time she'd checked the calendar, and despite the snow and the decorations, she wasn't ready for it to be Christmas quite yet.

Her kids had stopped asking if she wanted them home for Christmas years ago; she sent them Hanukkah presents every year, and they came home for Passover and Anna sometimes stayed a week or two. But watching everyone else's families come in late December always left Marianne a little bereft.

Kevin would probably call her Christmas morning, and she'd watch her usual X-Files marathon that night. Other than that, she'd been hoping Rana might want to have dinner since she didn't celebrate Christmas either. But now, Rana would be in her apartment across town tonight, and tomorrow she'd be a dozen yards away in her own shop, feeding the few residents of Swanley who either didn't celebrate Christmas, or who needed to escape their own families for a while.

Marianne's shop would be open a shortened day Christmas Eve—she was letting herself sleep in for a few hours and only opening after ten since very few people would be out and about that morning. She wouldn't bake much in the morning: mostly loaves of bread for people's Christmas dinners and the *pao de quiejo* filled with ham that she made every year for Ray and his snowplow crew. Word had gotten out about them, and now she had a whole fan club for them. She didn't make them year-round—people could drive into Framingham to get them from actual Brazilians—but on Christmas, she was the only *pao* game in town. She was somewhat glad there wouldn't be many customers—discussion the last few days had been all about the special election, and she was tired of worrying about it.

Instead, she pulled out a box from the closet and dusted it off, pulling the flaps open. Back before her mother died, they'd done big Christmases every year. She still had this box of stuff—all that was left of those celebrations. She started unpacking the box, each layer making her more nostalgic.

Here was the ornament she'd made in first grade, her handprint in some kind of clay and painted with red and green and circled with lace. And here was the blown-glass bird she'd never been allowed to touch, nestled in its wooden box that her mother's father had made by hand back in Greece. Beside it rested a small framed picture from her parents' wedding, a string attached with a plaque with their anniversary date in an etched heart. She picked it up, admiring her mother's wide tulle skirt and lace veil. Her father stood beside her, his face filled with joy. She hadn't seen that joy often after the war and after her mother died.

She'd never seen it on a picture of her and Kevin either. They'd married so young, been together so long, slowly sucking each other dry of the friendship and compassion they'd shared as kids, so by the time they'd divorced, they had nothing to say to each other. Only the last few years, after a decade avoiding each other, that they'd rekindled the friendship they should have kept all along. She wouldn't trade her kids for anything—the marriage had been worthwhile just for the three of them—but she wondered what a life would have been with someone she matched well. She hadn't dated anyone since the divorce, and only Tori before Kevin. That had been high school forty years ago. It was hard to admit, but she finally could—she was lonely. She missed having someone to share her life with—a teammate and partner. She could take or leave the naked parts—the companionship, ease, and love were what she missed most.

Marianne didn't know if Rana was that person for her. She didn't know if she'd ever get the chance to find out. But she wanted to try. She wanted a friend she'd made on her own terms, not one she'd known for forty years. Maybe if the whole situation with the deed and with Luke got resolved, there'd be less strangeness to fight through between the two of them. Because when they were together, when things were good, and no outside forces were adding stress and nonsense, everything was easy and fun between her and Rana. Attraction aside, she liked her. She liked her, and she wanted to be near her.

She poked the fire with the iron, watching the sparks drift around the burning logs. She'd figure this out. Maybe next December, they'd share the fire and the muffled sounds of carols, eating lo mein and watching Mulder and Scully. She hoped so.

*

Two days later, Marianne sat glued to the television. The forecast had called for snow, the day of the election, and Marianne had been hoping it would pass quickly or wear itself out over Albany or Springfield before it even got to Swanley. No such luck. By the evening, six inches had accumulated over twelve white mid-December hours, and voter turnout wasn't looking good. That didn't bode well for Ms. Hechevarria, Luke Leventi's opponent. Her supporters tended toward reliance on public transit or rides from friends, as well as trending young. And in a race between two Democrats whose policy differences weren't the huge chasm they'd be in states less liberal than Massachusetts, Marianne figured a lot of people probably looked outside and said *either one is good enough*.

She didn't usually stay up to watch the returns anymore, not the way she and Kevin had when they were young and certainly not the way they had when he was running for City Council. But tonight was different. The polls had to be wrong. He had sway, and he had connections, but people knew him. Swanley wouldn't elect Luke Leventi to represent them. There was no way.

As the returns began to trickle in, Marianne clutched her mug and pulled her blanket tighter around her. She'd voted early, dropping off her ballot weeks ago at city hall with each of the bubbles neatly filled in. That had been right when she and Rana had first been getting to know each other before she'd had any idea Luke was up to anything. She liked local elections: she knew everyone in them, knew most of them for decades as friends, neighbors, pro customers, and could vote accordingly. She didn't have to trust someone else's opinion or their public face; she knew what they looked like when the neighbor kid hit a ball through their window or when they got the wrong flavor in their coffee. She knew their moms and their kids and how well they tipped Zeke when he wasn't watching.

Part of her wished he'd taken Kevin up on his offer to let her join him to watch the returns at the Lucky Dog, but on the other hand, she wouldn't be able to watch in her pajamas there. And she'd be surrounded by his friends, former politicians, all of them, all reminiscing about the good old days when they ran the show.

She missed Rana fiercely, all of a sudden, missed her laugh and her smile and the way she made the things that panicked Marianne seem so easy to handle. Even with the awkwardness currently between them with the strange situation they were in, she wanted Rana there. In a few months she'd become a real friend, a part of Marianne's community. But Rana was away in California with her son, visiting while she recovered from the indignity of what the man currently winning the election had done to her business.

And he was winning, so far, with 20% reporting. All of Wilshire was in, going heavily for him, while Barchester was split evenly between him and his opponent with plenty left to report. Swanley, always the slowest town to submit their vote counts, wouldn't have all the votes counted until at least the morning. But the election would get called tonight, barring a very tight race. And she hoped it wouldn't be a nail-biter. Marianne didn't know if she could handle a nail-biter.

Another chunk of votes came in from precinct three in Swanley. The vote tipped back to Hechevarria, barely. "Come on," Marianne muttered into her tea as it cooled undrunk in her hands. "You know how awful he is." But she knew it wasn't likely Luke would lose. She knew how the slick suits, the good hair, the careful speeches, and the long history in the area played out with people who didn't have dealings with him. He looked good, and he sounded good, and that went a long way in Wiltshire County.

Another round of votes came in, the precinct to the farthest east, the only one in Dunbury. She always forgot that the district included a piece of Dunbury—from what she knew of the town, that wasn't a good thing for her candidate. He tended to play well in districts at opposite ends of the political spectrum—wealthy people who'd donated money and expected favors in return, and poor white areas where he made big promises. Those promises got him votes despite the unlikeliness that he would ever follow through.

I should have canvassed more, she thought, her mind starting to spiral as Yelena Hechevarria's lead shrunk a little more and then a little farther. They were even an hour and a half after polls had closed. It wouldn't be long now.

Her phone buzzed, and she set the tea down carefully before picking it up, opening the message from Zeke.

Can we close for mourning tomorrow if he wins?

She laughed out loud, a quick bark, as she typed back. *We'll spit in his coffee if he comes in.*

Zeke sent back a long row of tiny angry-faced emoji just as the political reporter for the local news, Karen Gilcrest, tapped her board, a checkmark appearing beside Luke Leventi onscreen.

"No," said Marianne. "What?" She stared at the little green mark. "That can't be right. He can't *win*."

She should have worked harder, should have donated more. She should have knocked on doors and done the phone bank. But she hadn't realized how much the election would matter back then. She hadn't realized what it would mean. So, she'd kind of ignored it all until the last month of the campaign. And by then it was too late.

If he was their representative, if he was the one controlling the laws, how could she win against him? How could she get Rana her shop back? And how could she kick that conniving asshole out of her family's business?

Chapter Sixteen

The mood in the library the next morning was mixed, some patrons somber, some quietly gleeful, some totally unaware anything had changed. Marianne brought her small stack of novels to the circulation desk, sharing a tired smile with Tori, whose familiar face looked drowsy behind the desk. "Late night?" she asked, taking in Tori's slight slump and large mug of coffee.

Tori shrugged. "Should have gone to bed," she said quietly. "What a mess."

"I stayed up until the end too. Zeke kept telling me to go to bed because I'd be useless in the morning. I swear knowing that kid is like having an extra mom. Or, a dad, I guess?"

"You can call him a mom," said Tori, laughing. "I don't think it's transphobic if you'd call a cis guy the same thing. How is that kid?"

Marianne smiled. "He's good," she said. "He's settling down with the classes and everything. I was worried he'd struggle and get overwhelmed, but he's handling it well. He's growing up, our Ezekiel."

"Tell him to come by," said Tori. "I haven't seen him lately. Makes me wonder if he only thinks I'm useful for trans lessons." She grinned wickedly. "If he were a little older, or I were a little shorter, it would have been perfect. I always wanted a trans man to switch wardrobes with. Instead, I got all the hard work of giving queer education without any of the payoff."

"What a great idea," said Marianne. "Somebody should set up some kind of pen pal thing like that."

"Oh, honey," said Tori. "The internet exists. Pen pal system, really?" She laughed. "Join the new millennium, Marianne." She shook her head. "You always were a dinosaur, all the way back."

"It's a good thing we broke up," said Marianne. "I'd have driven you crazy."

Tori laughed. "If I'd known you were bisexual in high school, I might not have dumped you when I finally admitted I was trans." She sighed, sobering. "And I might have been able to help out your new friend next door if I were around the bakery more often too."

"New friend?"

"Rana Wahbi," said Tori slyly. "The whole town's buzzing about you and her."

"Are you serious?" Marianne groaned. "There's nothing to buzz about, Tori!"

"Are you sure?" asked Tori. "You know how news travels around here. And I heard from Sandy at the bank that her daughter was in the restaurant and saw you all pink and giggly. I remember what you look like with a crush, my friend. People don't change. Not even in forty years." She held up both hands in a placating gesture. "But fine, you win. Nothing going on there. I'll mercilessly refute any further accusations of you having fun."

"You do that!" Marianne tried to look serious, but she was pretty sure she failed. "And what do you mean, help her out?"

Tori leaned closer, leaning her elbows on the counter. Her dark blue eyes leveled with Marianne's. "Our friend Mr. Leventi was in here last week," she said quietly. "Looking into local history. I thought it was kind of odd—

I knew he was trying for the House seat, of course, but he'd never showed any interest in history before then—but I figured he might be turning over a new leaf. But he took a call from his lawyer, I think, and was discussing—loudly, in the library, I might add—the terms of lease renewal."

"Well, that's clearly another reason people should have voted against him," joked Marianne, even as her stomach clenched. "Taking phone calls in the library."

Tori's eyes crinkled, for a second looking like the gorgeous kid Marianne had dated in high school, back before either of them realized they were queer. "More than just losing a vote. That should get you arrested."

"Impeached, maybe, now," said Marianne. "But I've been looking into history myself, and Tori, there's something fishy about the deed to the bakery."

"Fishiness?" Tori grinned. "You know I'm always up for some good fishiness. Spill."

"I don't really know anything yet," hedged Marianne. "But I'm not sure what exactly happened back when his dad took the property over. And I think I might have to figure it out to keep Rana in her shop."

"Oh, boy."

"I found a will my dad wrote," explained Marianne. "And now I don't know what to do. None of it makes sense, Tori. Least of all what's going on with Luke."

"Hm." Tori crossed her arms. "Well, he was certainly digging around. I'll let you know if he comes back, okay? He's not my favorite patron."

"Thanks, Tori. I really appreciate it. I think I set him on the warpath, and I'm not sure how to defuse him."

"I think you're right," said Tori, serious. "Be careful, honey."

"I always am, Tori."

Tori raised her eyebrows.

Marianne sighed. "I will be." She handed over the stack of books. "Now tell me about the kids. How have I not seen them all year?"

Tori's face lit up as she began recounting her twins' latest exploits. Marianne relaxed into the chatter, trying to put the previous topic of conversation out of her mind.

*

It was a little strange to be bringing Kevin and Rana into her apartment at the same time, and Marianne tried not to think about the fact that she'd kissed each of them on the same couch. She busied herself with turning up the thermostat as they entered, straightening stacks of papers on the counter and discreetly tossing a few old coffee cups in the trash before Kevin and Rana entered.

"Looks the same in here," said Kevin, glancing around. "Every time I come in, it surprises me. It's like snapping back to 1975."

"Some things are different," protested Marianne as she took Rana's coat and hung it in the closet. "There's a computer. And the fridge is new." Silence stretched for a long moment, and she cleared her throat. "Let's head to the living room, okay? I wanted to show this to you both."

Rana sat on the couch, while Kevin took the chair. Marianne pulled out the folder with the will and handed it to Kevin before sitting on the couch beside Rana. He opened the folder and set it on the coffee table. All three of them leaned in as Marianne flipped to the relevant section. She pointed, fingers hovering millimeters over the page.

"He didn't sell it, Kevin. Not according to this. Just like I said. There's nothing else that makes sense."

Kevin ran a hand through his hair. "Marianne, I stand by what I said before. You don't know that. You can't know it."

"Well neither do you!" Marianne's voice rose, and she could feel a lump forming in her throat. "Just because he wasn't all there doesn't mean he didn't know what was going on. He was depressed, not senile."

"He could have sold it afterward," Kevin said. "He could have meant the half he owned, if he sold it before. He could have been confused."

"You knew him?" asked Rana, leaning forward. "You knew Marianne's father well?"

Kevin nodded. "As well as anyone. He was my father-in-law, remember."

Rana half smiled. "I barely knew my father-in-law. Just because we were family didn't mean we knew each other well."

"Well, I knew Danny," said Kevin sharply. "And he wasn't the most careful man in the world, especially not with paperwork."

Marianne put a hand on Rana's wrist, stilling her objections. "The will is real, Kevin. He wrote this. I knew my father better than you did, remember."

He tipped his head slightly in acknowledgment.

"So, what do we do with it? Who do we tell?"

"Assuming we're able to confirm it as a legal will?"

"Okay, Kevin, we're not lawyers. Start from the beginning. How do we do that?"

He smiled. "Well, first things first. You're going to have to get a lawyer."

Marianne waved at him. "We have a lawyer."

Kevin laughed. "No, you don't. We talked about that."

Rana shook her head. "Your former husband cannot be your lawyer, Marianne," Rana said quietly. "Believe me, that's a recipe for disaster."

"She's right," said Kevin. "I can help you hire someone else, and I can help out with advice, but no, that would be a serious conflict of interest." He tapped his fingers on the wood of the table as the headlights from a passing car cast a flickering beam of light across his pale features. "I was thinking about Lila Shapiro, actually."

Marianne blinked. "Tori's wife?"

Kevin nodded. "She takes cases like this—well, not *like* this, this one is particularly weird—but property cases and inheritance disputes and things like that."

Marianne glanced at Rana, who shrugged. "I don't think I know her," confessed Rana.

"She has the twins," said Marianne. "They're about eight? The boy loves trains and the girl is autistic?"

"Oh!" Rana brightened. "And she has a very tall wife?"

Marianne grinned. "That's Tori. Yes."

"I didn't realize she was a lawyer," said Rana.

"She is," said Kevin. "A damn good one too. She usually takes cases out in Boston and Worcester, but she interned with Dougie way back when."

"Kevin's cousin. Also a lawyer," explained Marianne to Rana.

"She'd be willing to represent you at a discount as a favor to us, I'm sure. Or even pro bono. She and Tori certainly don't like Luke Leventi much either."

"And they'd hate to see the bakery go," added Rana.

"I hate to ask," said Marianne.

"Would you rather lose the bakery when Leventi gets his way?" asked Kevin.

"Well, no, but—"

"That's what's going to happen if we don't do something."

Marianne looked from one to the other and then around at the old walls of the bakery apartment, thick with memories. "Okay. I'll go talk to Tori tomorrow, ask her for Lila's work number."

Chapter Seventeen

Marianne wasn't sure why the idea of asking Lila Shapiro to be her lawyer was making her so nervous. Maybe it was the fact that when it was just Kevin and Rana and her discussing the will, it was all nothing but a theoretical discussion between friends. But once she asked a lawyer—one she'd hire, rather than one she was badgering with questions—she was really doing this.

Or maybe it was that she'd always been a little nervous around Lila. She was nearly fifteen years younger than Marianne and Tori, after all, and despite forty years' distance, Marianne was still Lila's wife's ex. It would be ridiculous for Lila to think of her as a threat. She and Tori had broken up in the 1970s and had both been so deep inside their respective straight camouflages back then as to be nearly unrecognizable. And Lila had never given her any reason to be nervous.

But she had to admit, deep down, part of her wondered what would have happened had she and Tori stayed together through the revelations of their respective queernesses. Could they have worked their relationship out? And even though she thought of Tori as a friend now, a good friend, there would always be that tiny little spark of *what if*.

She pushed open the door to the library and stepped inside, breathing in the faint scents of paper and surreptitiously smuggled coffee. The main reading room was mostly deserted this early in the morning, and Tori was nowhere in sight. Behind the desk sat Michaela, the reference librarian, reading a thick paperback with gold foil glinting on the cover. She looked up as Marianne approached.

"What can I do for you?" she asked, sticking a scrap of paper in the book and setting it down.

"Is Tori in today?" asked Marianne. "I need to ask her something."

"She's around here somewhere," said Michaela. "Can I help?"

"It's personal, sorry," said Marianne.

Michaela's eyebrows rose behind her thick glasses and her gaze sharpened. "Personal?"

"Well, it's somewhat professional, I guess" clarified Marianne, "But not library-related."

"Hm," said Michaela, and Marianne groaned internally. Michaela was an incorrigible gossip. Ten years younger than Marianne, she'd been one of the kids Marianne had babysat as a teen. She'd been nosy then, and she was nosy now. "I think she's shelving over by mysteries."

"Thanks," said Marianne. She felt Michaela's eyes follow her the whole way back through the stacks until she turned the corner and was out of sight.

Michaela had been right—Tori knelt in the *T* section of science fiction, just past the edge of the mysteries. Marianne knocked a low-hanging novel from the shelf as she passed, sending the book clattering to the floor, and Tori started, nearly falling over backward.

"Sorry," said Marianne, catching her by the shoulder as she pushed herself upright. She picked up the novel she'd dropped and smiled at the familiar cover. "Been a long time since I read Dune," she admitted, pushing it back between Heinlein and Huxley. "I didn't mean to startle you."

Tori laughed. "That's all right. Can I help you find something?"

"I was looking for you, actually."

Tori raised her eyebrows. "Me?"

"Well. Your wife."

"You won't find Lila here," said Tori, grinning. "She says she hears enough about this place at home. She wouldn't be caught dead hanging out here with all the stories I tell." She leaned in. "Did I tell you about what we found on the floor last week when we closed?"

"Do I want to know?"

Tori grimaced. "Probably not. Let's just say we're going to put up more signs for the bathrooms."

"Someone—oh, no." Marianne shook her head. "Nope, I don't believe that. No one could be that gross."

"Michaela's theory is that it was a political statement." Tori shrugged. "They went right in front of the climate change display."

Marianne giggled. "That's horrible."

"And *that* is why Lila doesn't come by," Tori concluded. "You, on the other hand, have been a frequent visitor lately. So, tell me, what can my lovely wife do for you?"

Marianne sighed. "I need a lawyer, Tori."

Tori cocked her head to one side, crossing her arms. "What did you do, Marianne? Toilet papered another house after all these years?"

"You know that wasn't me," said Marianne. "That was you and Teddy and Ray. Forty years later, and you're still trying to pin it on me." She shook her head. "No, it's for the bakery. For the thing with the property."

"Oh!" Tori nodded. "I was telling her about that. She seemed pretty interested. You know she loves all that town history stuff." She smiled. "And she loves the bakery."

"Well, there's been some new developments," said Marianne. "We found a will from my dad that raises some questions, and Kevin says he can't be my lawyer to try to get it verified, or official, or whatever needs to happen to it. Probate, he said."

Tori nodded. "Makes sense. You and Kevin get along well enough. Safer not to add anything new and complicated to that if it's working."

"I guess."

"What?"

"It's just—this is all a lot more complicated than I thought it would be."

Tori glanced up at the clock and started back toward the desk and Marianne followed. "My lunch break's coming up. How about we grab a salad, and you tell me about it?"

Marianne nodded. "I'm buying though."

Tori smiled. "I won't argue with that. Hey, Michaela?" she called toward the desk as they passed.

Michaela glanced over, her cheeks warm, pulling her eyes from the man sitting on the other side of the desk. He had one hand over hers and released her fingers when she looked up. "Yeah?"

"Going to lunch. See you in an hour." Tori grabbed her coat from under the printer table. "Call if you need backup. We'll be right down the street."

"Got it, boss," said Michaela, already back in conversation. The man looked familiar, but Marianne couldn't place him. Somebody's brother, probably, someone she'd known in passing. In a small town, everyone was related to someone you knew.

*

Marianne had never been to Lila Shapiro's office. She wasn't surprised to find the room as sharply neat as Lila herself, all squared corners and polished wood and brass. She even had one of those green desk lamps she'd expect to see in a bank. If she hadn't been a friend of the family, there was no way Marianne would be able to afford her.

"So the first thing we're going to need to do is file this in probate," said Lila, leaning back in her chair. "Until we do that, it's nothing but old paper."

Marianne smoothed the folder down, its edges fuzzy with age though she'd wiped it down to get rid of fifty years of dust. Her fingers brushed her father's handwriting on the tab, tracing the letters. "That's what Kevin said."

"Now that's a couple forms that we have to fill out and then bring to the courthouse. They'll take the will and give us a copy; then we can start looking into the situation. You said there's some debate over the sale of the part of the property that's now the Cairo Grill?"

"That's right," said Marianne. "According to this, I don't think my father actually sold it. And we can't find any record of a sale in the town archives."

Lila grinned, teeth sharp and white. Marianne had never seen this side of her, this professional, laser-focused side. She'd only see the side Lila showed around her kids and Tori—the warm, smilingly competent maternal side. This was different. She'd always been cute, but Marianne had a sudden new appreciation for Tori's choice of wife. This was a woman who could hold her own in any situation she wanted to. "If that's true, we're going to make sure he pays. Not just for the original trick—for all the years of rent he should have been turning over to you."

Marianne gulped.

She called Kevin the next morning to catch him up on the situation. She could usually count on him being home Saturday mornings—he'd always liked to have a leisurely time with the paper on the weekends. The phone rang long enough that she'd begun to wonder if he'd changed his routine, but he finally picked up, a little out of breath.

"Hey, Kevin," she said.

"Marianne!" He said, sounding surprised. "What's going on? Is it the kids?"

"No!" She rushed to reassure him. "I wanted to tell you about meeting with Lila. Is this a bad time?"

"Uh, no," he replied. "So, you officially hired her?"

"Yes, but I'd like your input. I can head over in a couple minutes, if you're decent. I'll make you coffee, and bring over those scones you like, with the bacon in them."

"No!" Kevin's response was quick. "No, I'll come by. Is this afternoon okay?"

Marianne paused. A sneaking suspicion was rising in her. "Kevin?" she asked.

"Yes, Marianne." He sounded resigned.

"Do you have someone over there?"

"What?"

She grinned. "A *special visitor*? You picked up some lonely single lady on a Friday night, didn't you?"

"No!" Kevin's response was louder than before, and he cut himself off and lowered his voice. "No, I didn't! No ladies here, nope."

"Oh, come on." She thought for a minute, a slow smile spreading over her face. "Kevin?"

"Yes?"

"Did you pick *someone* up last night and have them spend the night?"

Silence on the other end.

"Oh my god. Kevin, did you pick up a guy last night?"

The silence stretched.

Marianne waited him out.

Finally, Kevin said quietly, "Maybe."

Marianne tried not to laugh because she didn't want Kevin to think she was laughing *at* him. Thirty years together—more than that, actually—and deep down she'd always thought he was just as bisexual as she was, with his Tom Cruise fixation and his shirtless James Bond artwork in the rec room. No, she was laughing in delight and vindication. Only she really couldn't start laughing out loud because Kevin's pride probably wouldn't take it, and this call was, originally, to ask him a favor.

"All right," she said instead, stifling her glee. Of course, two queer people would have married each other. Of course, they'd have been drawn to each other back then. And, of course, it fell apart under the weight of their own individual closet-case neuroses. "Well, I'm happy you had a nice evening." She paused. "You did have a nice time, right?"

"Yes," Kevin admitted. His voice held a surprising shyness. "I did." He cleared his throat. "And I'm not telling you anything else, because this conversation is already weird enough."

"That's definitely fine," said Marianne. "I'll see you this afternoon then? I can give you the update, and you can at least tell me what you think I should do?"

"I will," said Kevin. "Just give me a few hours."

She laughed aloud this time, finally, and thanked him again, promised to make a batch of peanut butter cookies as well in payment, and then hung up the phone.

So Kevin was bi, too, or at least a little bit queer; however he chose to identify when he got that figured out. What would that have meant if he'd been able to explore that while they were married? Sometimes she wondered if things would have worked out better had they been in a different generation, one where conversations about the spectrum of sexuality and gender were more open and nuanced than they had been in her and Kevin's suburban 1970s childhoods.

At least her kids didn't have the same societal damage she and Kevin had had to overcome. The three of them could be who they were, whatever that turned out to be. None of them were settled yet—Anna was dating a person whose pronouns and chosen name were currently in flux, and Janie had just dumped that Rudy guy the previous August and had been dating a new girl for the past few months—but they knew that whoever they brought home to Swanley, their identity wouldn't cause trouble at home. Although given Jacob's affinity for women who walked off with expensive items from his apartment, never to be seen again, she reserved the right to be skeptical of his potential romantic partners.

And she wondered, too, if all the new conversations about the asexual spectrum would have changed things. Maybe knowing there was a name for how she felt would have made it easier to manage Kevin and her mismatched libidos and make their relationship work. But maybe not. They were better friends than they'd ever been spouses, even if he drove her up the wall sometimes.

Marianne closed the apartment door behind her, finally heading down to the bakery to get the ovens going for the day's baked goods. As she rolled out dough, she thought about Rana.

If she and Kevin hadn't divorced, she certainly wouldn't have met Rana in the way she did. She would have been living miserably out in the big house on West Springfield while Rana shivered alone in the Cairo Grill with no heat and no electricity the day of the big storm. Or she might have tried to drive home, and something terrible might have happened.

Marianne shivered, casting the thought aside. She had been there, and she and Rana had clicked in a way Marianne hadn't with anyone in years, maybe ever. Certainly not since those first few years with Kevin, if even then. It was so long ago, now, and she found it hard to dredge the feeling she'd had back then. And the angst was all so mixed up in the expectations around her dad and the bakery, and her dad's depression and health issues, she wasn't sure where one ended and the next began.

She liked Rana. They'd only known each other a short time, but somehow it felt longer. Rana knew her ex-husband, and she'd met Rana's daughter. They'd spent hours and hours together, and though they'd clashed occasionally, the spark had been palpable. And it was new, the thing they'd had; it didn't have the strings that tugged back through her life, pulling on all the pieces of herself she'd shed as she'd aged. She and Rana had met as the fully formed people they were now—capable of change, still growing, but not deep in the trenches of figuring out who they were.

She slid a tray of cookies into the big oven and then a rack of bread into the other one. She needed to stop dwelling on Rana, and what could have been. And all the problems with Leventi and the suit could wait until the afternoon and Kevin's visit. She turned on the radio and tried to focus on the croissants. At least she'd gotten to sleep in somewhat—she didn't know if she could have dealt with any of this after waking up at three in the morning.

*

When Kevin finally slunk into the bakery around two thirty in the afternoon, Marianne was busy with a family of tourists looking for directions back to the highway. She saw him out of the corner of her eye and finished handing the adults their coffee and making sure they had a clear idea of where they were supposed to be going. Finally, they headed back out to the street. She hoped they'd find their way. She wasn't confident they would. But that left her and Kevin alone in the bakery.

He avoided her eyes, focusing on the paper he'd grabbed off another table, until she set a mug of coffee in front of him.

"It's decaf," she informed him. "You look like you've got enough anxiety without the caffeine giving it a boost."

He took the coffee and leaned back in his chair. "What did you want to tell me?" He asked, clearing his throat.

Marianne smiled. She'd had a feeling he'd want to ignore the subject of his night. Kindly, she let him get away with it. "Lila's going to help me file the will," she said. "And she said we're going to sue him too. If we can prove he's not the owner, then he owes me all the rent he's charged."

"She sounds like she's doing a good job," said Kevin. He took another long sip of coffee. "The will first, though, right?"

"Yeah. We're going to head over to the courthouse tomorrow and see if we can get the paperwork filed. Once that happens, we can get more information." She considered him for a moment. "You look good, Kevin."

He glanced up at her, meeting her eyes, and smiled. "Do I?"

"Except the bags under your eyes from what looks like a late night, yes. You could have told me, you know. If anyone wasn't going to judge you for being interested in men, it'd be me."

He sighed, drumming his fingers on the coffee mug. "I know that."

"So why didn't you say anything? I mean, other than it being none of my business after we got divorced."

He shook his head. "I don't know, Marianne. I guess I wasn't ever sure. I had you, and I'd always been with women, and being with men seemed—I don't know, unnecessary. Complicated. Difficult. I didn't need anyone else because there were plenty of women in my life. It never came up, I guess."

"And now?"

He shrugged. "I was at PJ's last night. I started talking about the Patriots with a guy I'd never seen around town. Things escalated from there when PJ's closed."

"You had fun though?"

Marianne was delighted to see Kevin's cheeks pink. "Yes."

"Well." She patted his hand. "I'm glad. Only took you sixty years, but I'm glad."

Chapter Eighteen

At least she knew no legal nonsense on the other side would be happening over Christmas either. Lila had warned her it would be unlikely they could file the will before the county closed for the holiday, and she'd been right. So, they'd set a date of December 26th to meet at the courthouse, and Marianne tried not to stress herself too much about it.

Christmas Day, she always opened the bakery, though she gave herself a few hours off in the morning like the day before. She opened around eleven, and her first customers wandered in a half hour or so later as she pulled a tray of blueberry muffins off the cooling racks to set in the display case.

"Just a minute!" she called from the oven around the corner. "I'll be right there!"

"It's fine," called a familiar voice from the store. "Take your time!"

Marianne hurried back around the corner with the tray, smiling at Tori and Lila and their twins, who sat at a table kicking their feet. The kids had to be at least eight now, though Marianne couldn't imagine how they could be so big already. She remembered when they were born, Tori agonizing over whether she was too old to be a mom at fifty-two, and Lila joking that she was one of the only lesbians in the world who could have a baby genetically related to both her and her wife. It seemed like a few months ago, not nearly a decade. "Hi, guys!"

Tori stepped closer, leaning in. "We promised them baked goods," she said conspiratorially. "They know all their friends are getting presents right now for Christmas."

"Hanukkah wasn't enough for them?" asked Marianne.

"Hanukkah ended two weeks ago," said Lila. "They've already forgotten it."

"Well, you don't see their friends out here getting to pick muffins, do you?"

Tori grinned. "Exactly." She turned. "Sarah, Davey, you want to come pick something from Miss Marianne?"

Davey sprang up and ran over, nearly knocking over a table on the way. Sarah followed a little more sedately, face serious.

"Hi, David. Hi, Sarah," said Marianne. She bent down a little to meet Davey's eyes. "What would you like today?"

"A chocolate one!" He pointed at the croissants. When Lila cleared her throat meaningfully, he added, "Please? And Sarah wants a muffin."

"Sarah, do you want blueberry or cranberry?"

Sarah stared at a point behind Marianne's head and stood on her tiptoes to look through the glass and then dropped back down, considering. After a moment, she pointed at the blueberry ones.

"She wants blueberry," said Davey.

"They might be a little hot. Is that okay?"

Sarah nodded. Marianne grinned. "Great! Let me get you those." She looked up at Tori and Lila. "And coffee for the grownups?"

"God, yes," said Lila. "Huge coffees."

"Enormous," Tori agreed.

Marianne laughed. "Coming right up."

Since there was no one else waiting, Marianne made herself a coffee as well and brought the food and coffees out on a tray instead of calling for pickup from the counter. "Sit with us a few minutes?" asked Tori, patting the seat beside her. "I haven't seen you lately, not as much as Lila's gotten to."

Marianne glanced at Lila, who smiled and waved at the seat. "We'd love to have you join us," she said.

"I don't want to interrupt your family time," said Marianne. "Especially now that I'm Lila's client."

Tori rolled her eyes. "No talking about the legal stuff, and we'll be fine." She patted the seat again.

"All right," said Marianne. "How's the library?"

Tori shrugged. "Same old place," she said. "Caught some kids trying to sneak a bottle of wine into the Russian lit section. Reminded me of old times." She smiled at Lila. "Marianne and I used to hide out in the library sometimes, back in the day. Remember the time we snuck in a whole pie?"

Marianne laughed. "I can't believe they hired you."

"All the librarians who knew my secrets had already retired. So, no one suspected me." She waggled her brows. "Especially once I transitioned. The perfect crime!"

"Tori tells some good stories about the two of you," said Lila, laughing. "You were quite the pair."

"Couldn't last," said Tori, leaning over to kiss her wife's cheek. "I had to dump Marianne to find you."

Lila chuckled. "Since I was a toddler when the two of you dated, it's for the best."

The bell over the door chimed as another couple walked in, looking damp and bedraggled, and with a quick goodbye to the Shapiros, Marianne got up to usher them toward the counter.

"See you tomorrow," Lila called as Marianne slid behind the pastry case. "Don't forget the paperwork."

*

Boxing Day dawned cloudy and gray, warm enough for the slush to melt but not enough for anyone to be comfortable. After the quick drive across the border into Wilshire, Marianne parked in the county lot and walked the two blocks to the county court complex.

The probate court was held in a grubby little building off the main courthouse. Marianne had just paused on the steps, turning to look back the way she came, when a voice startled her from much nearer than she was comfortable with.

"Marianne." Luke Leventi stood less than ten feet behind her in a dark suit, a manila envelope in his hand. "Fancy seeing you here," he said.

"It's not nice to sneak up on a woman," said Marianne, trying to calm her racing heart. "Or anyone, really."

He shrugged. "It's not nice to try to steal someone's business either, but here we are."

"Steal your business? What?"

He smiled.

As her eyes met his, Marianne noted the dark patches under his eyes and the slight looseness of his usually perfectly tied tie. His shoes were still perfectly polished, reflecting the sunlight, and his shirt had a subtle blush color against the dark gray pinstripe of his suit. Even angry and stressed, the man could dress.

"My property. It's brought in business for you, too, having that suite working next door to you. That would have fallen by the wayside, wasted space, if my father had left it in your father's hands. Look how few customers you get in your shop."

"It's not like they have any parking," snapped Marianne. And you haven't exactly managed to keep businesses going over there, have you? Rana's the tenant you've had the longest in decades, if I recall correctly. I'm not sure why you'd give that up by kicking her out—she's the only one who's made that space work."

He snorted, a jarring sound out of his put-together appearance, and one that reminded her he didn't grow up in the fancy suits and well-bred manners he liked to posture in these days. "I don't give a shit about the restaurant," he said. "I care about you screwing up my deal to sell it."

"You're trying to ruin my life and Rana's too. You don't think I'm going to take that, do you, Luke? I would have thought after fifty years you'd know me better than that."

He shrugged, sliding his hands into his pockets. "You wanted to look into this mess, fine. We can do that. My dad might have bought that place, he might not. Either way, it's mine now. You won't be getting it back. And neither will your Egyptian friend. She'll be gone. And in a year or so, once the Dunkin' is up and running with their dollar coffees and sixty-five cent donuts, backed up by CoffeeGuru and their delivery scooters all around town, you'll be begging to sell."

"Sell?" Marianne laughed. "Luke, I'm never going to sell to you. You should know that right now."

"No?" His smile widened. "Are you sure about that?" He glanced behind her at the building and then over toward the train station down the road. "Did your property taxes seem a little higher this year, Marianne?"

They had, but Marianne wasn't going to give him the satisfaction of a yes.

"We've had a huge influx of commuters over in Wilshire, did you know that? Folks who think that forty-five minutes on the train is a great deal for rural living. And folks who aren't going to get their coffee from a crappy local shop that's falling apart at the seams. If they don't come by my Dunkin', or order through CoffeeGuru, they'll hit the Starbucks in South Station and whine about the lines. In a few years, this piece of land will be so expensive your flagging profits won't be able to pay the tax bills anymore. I can help you, if you'd rather do this that way."

"What do you mean, help me?"

He shrugged. "We can make some kind of a deal."

Marianne let out a bark of laughter. "I don't think so. You try anything, and I'll see you in court, asshole."

He shrugged. "That's Representative Asshole, to you. And fine. See you there. It's all the same to me. You'll sell when you're broke from legal fees just as easy as broke from property taxes." He turned. "See you around, Marianne."

She stood on the steps, shaking with adrenaline, as he slid into his car and pulled away. Then she carefully climbed the steps, leaned her shoulder against the wall, covered her face, and took a moment to pull herself together.

It took longer than she'd expected, residual stress making her heart pound and her hands shake. She tried to breathe deeply, her breath catching in her throat and a low tingling in her belly, cold trickling down her spine. Finally, she swallowed hard and straightened her dress, pushing into the building. As she came through the doors, she found Lila inside the vestibule typing on her phone. She looked up when Marianne came in, nodding a hello distracted and then glanced more closely at Marianne, face softening a little into concern. "Hey," she said. "It's going to be all right."

Marianne pulled her coat tighter around her. "This seems like a lot of fuss that might open a big can of worms."

"Second thoughts?"

Marianne sighed. "I'm not sure, Lila. I don't want to make things worse."

"How much worse will they get without you doing this?" asked Lila. "Because it sounds to me like you're going to lose your bakery to Dunkin' Donuts if you don't do something."

"I hate having to choose between two bad choices; that's all," said Marianne. She didn't want to tell Lila about Luke's veiled threats. It was just talk, after all. "I hate being forced into action."

"I get that," said Lila. "I really do. But you know, this is righting a wrong. You shouldn't have to do this, but once you do, it'll be as your dad wanted it—you in charge of the family business, not some sneaky interloper."

"I guess."

"Are you ready to go in?"

Marianne swallowed hard and clutched the accordion folder holding the will and deed closer. "All right."

Lila grinned and led her up the steps and in the main entrance to the courthouse proper, stamping her feet on the mat inside to knock off the caked slush. Marianne followed suit. The building was relatively empty, though they could hear a muffled argument through the thin walls to their left. Marianne followed Lila through a short maze of hallways to a winding set of stanchions and up to a long desk where a clerk sat clacking away on a keyboard. Lila paused in the doorway for a moment, taking a deep breath and then continued in. The woman looked up as they stopped in front of her.

"Hello, Gloria," said Lila, smiling carefully at the small woman behind the desk. The woman stopped typing, turning to them.

"Ms. Shapiro," she said, voice stiff. "What can I do for you?"

"We're here to file a will," said Lila, holding out a hand to Marianne. "It's for an estate settled in the eighties. It's 121 Main Street in Swanley."

Gloria picked up a pair of bright pink reading glasses and set them on her nose, glancing at Marianne over them. "Hmm, 121 Main Street, is it?" She took the folder, flipping it open and pulling out the form Marianne and Lila had spent the evening perfecting. Her eyes darted down the spread pages and then back up at Lila and Marianne. "There's a problem here. I can tell you that already." She shook her head. "Somebody beat you to it."

"Beat us to it?" Marianne shook her head. "This is the only copy. There was no other will."

"Oh, they didn't file a will," said Gloria. "They challenged this one."

"But we hadn't even brought it in yet!"

Gloria pulled her glasses back off, letting them dangle on the chain around her neck. "That doesn't matter, honey."

"Who filed a challenge?" asked Lila, though Marianne knew the answer already.

Gloria typed another string into her computer and then looked up. "Lucas Leventi. Just this morning."

"That's what he was doing!" Burst out Marianne. "I just saw him," she explained to Lila. "Outside, on my way in. He was hinting about something, trying to get me to sell him the whole building."

Lila's mouth thinned into a tight line. "All right. We can weather this." She turned back to the desk. "Gloria, is there a date set yet for the trial?"

"Trial?" asked Marianne.

"He's contesting the will," explained Lila. "Usually people wait until after it's filed in probate, but this is, unfortunately, legal. We have to meet in court to figure it out."

Gloria's eyebrows rose. "It's scheduled as of this morning. In a week."

"A week?" Lila said, astonished. "That's impossible! Nothing moves that fast around here."

Gloria shrugged. "It does when the person initiating the challenge got elected to the House. Representative Leventi knows how to work the system. You know that."

Lila tipped her head up, sighing heavily. "All right. Looks like we've got some work ahead of us."

*

When Marianne pushed open the door to the bakery, Zeke looked up from the register and grinned. "Just took a catering order for sixty muffins," he called as he handed a woman a tea. "For next Friday. Some kind of fundraiser."

"That's great, Zeke," Marianne replied distractedly. "Give me a couple minutes, and I'll come relieve you, all right? I know you've been stuck here a lot lately, and I appreciate it."

He shrugged. "I'm fine here, and I need the overtime. Take your time. I'm saving up for a new phone."

Marianne thanked him and headed around the building to update Rana. She'd seen her once with Kevin since she'd gotten back from her trip, and once through the window as she walked by the bakery, but they hadn't had a moment to have a real conversation alone since the news about Rana's lease. Marianne's stomach burned, unsettled with anxiety as she trudged through the snow.

If I win this and somehow own both sides of the building, I'm putting a door back in between the suites, she said to herself and then pushed the thought down. She didn't want to jinx herself by planning for an outcome she wasn't sure was even possible. And she didn't want to think of herself as Rana's landlord; that was for sure.

As Marianne wiped her feet on the mat inside the Cairo Grill, Rana appeared from the kitchen. Her face lit up when she saw Marianne.

Rana's eyes were beautiful, dark brown and wide with scattered crow's-feet fanning out from the corners, and her smile drove deep dimples into her cheeks. Marianne smiled back, warmth coalescing in her chest. All nonsense about legal things and all the awkwardness of their aborted relationship aside, she liked Rana. She just did. She liked her humor and her food and her smile, and she liked the way Rana had somehow gotten to know everyone in town so quickly. It made her realize a little how isolated she'd become—seeing Rana laughing with customers like they were old friends, customers Marianne had known her whole life and wasn't that open with. But Rana, in only a few months, was part of Swanley. "Hi," she said, suddenly a little uncomfortable.

"Hi," said Rana. "I heard there was news."

Marianne blinked. "You heard already?"

Rana laughed. "Ray was in earlier. He said his sister-in-law works at the courthouse and saw you and Lila coming out looking angry."

"Even in Wilshire I can't get away from the gossip network," grumbled Marianne. "But it's not good news. I'm sorry to say."

"I didn't expect it to be good. Sit," said Rana. "I've got a few minutes. You know I don't usually have many afternoon customers."

"I can't stay long," said Marianne. "I left Zeke with a line." She slid onto a stool, sighing as her weight shifted off her feet. She wasn't used to wearing business casual like she'd decided to do for the trip to the courthouse. Making a good impression might not be worth wearing fancy boots. "Leventi is suing us."

"He's what?"

"Well, not us. The will, I think? I didn't quite understand what he's doing, but the point is, we have to go to court to prove my dad's will is valid." She shook her head. "I hate this."

Rana reached over and placed her hand on Marianne's forearm, hers cool and dry through Marianne's sleeve. "I do too. But we're going to fight it."

"We are," said Marianne. "We don't have a choice."

Rana laughed a little. "When you put it that way, it sounds less noble, Marianne." The door whined as it opened, letting in a group of chattering teens. "I have customers," she said apologetically. "Let me know how I can help."

Marianne nodded. "Thank you. I will."

*

Marianne hadn't taken out her only business-like dress in years—not since her cousin Lydia's funeral in 2012. And she had had a suit at one point, but she hadn't seen it since the late nineties. Even if the outfit was still lurking somewhere in her closet, it was unlikely to fit anymore, or be in style. She'd gotten by for years in long skirts and blouses on the few occasions she'd needed something more formal than jeans and less fun than her blue dress. She sighed heavily, staring into her closet.

Lila had told her she had to dress nicely, but not too nicely. Professional, not attention-grabbing. They'd spent nearly as much time on demeanor as they had on the actual will. That had mostly been Lila, the legal end of it—the will was witnessed by two signatures, and Lila had found other documents signed by the same old military buddies of Marianne's father to match up to the witness signatures. It would have been better if one of them had been alive, but no such luck.

Getting ready for the paperwork side of court had been one thing. Now facing the actual day in front of a real judge, she froze.

It doesn't matter what you wear, she thought to herself. You've done nothing wrong, and they'll see that.

But Luke Leventi was always so put together, looking sleek and masculine in suits and ties, almost presidential. Kevin was the same way, and for a moment, she wondered if she should have called her ex-husband for fashion advice. But that was a ridiculous thought, and she cast it aside as fast as it occurred. She had no interest in inviting him into her bedroom, even for something this innocuous.

Rana always looked good, she thought, closing the door. Maybe she could ask her.

Her chest warmed and she closed her eyes, trying not to freak herself out with the thought. So, they'd kissed and spent a night together on the couch. So what? If Rana had wanted more, she would have said something by now. They were friends these days. Marianne didn't even know if she wanted more. It was so rare that she did. Friendship was easier. Friendship was great. And Marianne didn't exactly have a lot of friends. She was happy to have Rana in that capacity. It wasn't less than dating. It was just different, and if Marianne was honest with herself, maybe not quite what she wanted.

Rana was smart and gorgeous and thoughtful a great cook, something Marianne had never expected to find in a friend. She was always the cook in any relationship, friendship or otherwise. Owning a bakery kind of guaranteed that. Spending time with Rana and getting to have new, delicious things brought to her by a beautiful woman? She saw the appeal.

She pulled on her coat and trudged outside, shivering in the biting wind, though it felt good to cool off her burning face. She needed to shove this crush down further, if she didn't want to make Rana uncomfortable. A sudden thought occurred to her—Rana had never seen her bedroom. If she invited her up to help her dress, it would be in her bedroom, next to her bed. They'd walk right by the couch they'd spent their one evening of intimacy on. She had to pull herself together.

Marianne was too old for this nonsense. She peered into Rana's front door, squinting through the dark room. She hadn't realized how late it was. The shop was closed. Rana was probably long gone. She stood there another moment and then turned back to the slushy sidewalk. She had just begun walking through another particularly chilly gust of wind when a burst of warmth and sound behind her made her turn back around.

"Marianne?" called a familiar voice. "Is that you?" Rana stood in the doorway, shivering in a thin sweater, and Marianne felt a broad smile spill over her face. "Come inside!" Called Rana. "You're letting all the heat out."

Marianne followed the warm smell of bread and lamb through the door, letting out a deep breath of relief as the warmth of Rana's shop enveloped her. "Sorry to bother you," she said as Rana shut and locked the door behind her, leading her into the room behind the big sinks across the back counter. She hadn't been back here in years, maybe even decades, and it was so strange to see how completely different Rana had made the room from the way the previous tenants had arranged it. Neat stacks of paper lay across a modern brushed metal desk, a wooden rolling chair that looked older than either of them tucked in behind it. A framed black and white photo of a cityscape, the tip of a pyramid cresting over skyscrapers, hung on the wall behind the bookshelves.

"I must apologize for the mess," said Rana. "I was doing the accounting. But it's warmer back here, and no customers can see us and think we're open for business. They'll leave instead."

"Like I nearly did," said Marianne smiling. "Sorry to bother you."

"You're not a customer." Rana's cheeks dimpled. "Don't worry."

"A customer would buy things," replied Marianne, but she settled into the overstuffed loveseat across the back of the office. "I enjoy what you give me for free."

"I'm happy to feed my friends," said Rana. "Besides, you do the same for me." She pulled the chair out and settled in it, "What can I do for you? Or is this just a social call? Because I'm happy for the company if so."

Marianne laughed. "I wish," she said. "No, I need fashion advice."

"Fashion advice?" Rana chucked. "That's a new one."

"Well, I have court in the morning."

"Oh." Rana sobered. "I remember."

"And I never go anywhere formal," Marianne sighed. "I'm not sure what I'm even supposed to wear to court." She shook her head. "I just need another set of eyes, really." She paused, butterflies in her stomach. "Would you mind coming up and helping me sort through my options?"

Rana glanced over at the computer screen and then back at Marianne. A smile broke over her face, dimpling her cheeks and creasing the lines around her eyes. "That would be much better than bookkeeping." She clicked to save the file and then stood, sliding her feet into boots and throwing a jacket over her shoulders. "I'll be over in a few minutes—I need to finish a few things up here first, all right?"

Marianne nodded, levering herself out of her own seat. "I'll leave the side door to the apartment unlocked. You remember how to get in?"

Rana gave her a long look, and Marianne's cheeks heated. Of course she did. She'd been there three times, and if that first night was half as memorable to Rana as it was to Marianne, she remembered every inch of that stairwell and the room beyond it. "I do," said Rana finally. There was a note of something in her voice, something secret and odd. Marianne nodded and headed back out into the cold and around to the side door of her apartment, the one that didn't require her to go through the bakery. She'd had the new entrance installed when she'd moved back in after the divorce, and it had been one of the best decisions she'd made: not having to traipse through the bakery every time she needed to leave her house was a huge improvement to both her convenience and her building's fire code adherence.

She wiped her feet carefully, hanging her coat on the peg in the tiny mudroom at the base of the stairs and then shed her boots and climbed the steps up to her front door. The stairwell was chilly without her coat, and she enjoyed the sudden warmth as she slipped back into her cozy living room. She looked around the space with a critical eye, suddenly aware of the blanket crumpled in the corner of the couch, the empty plate by the sink, the sweater tossed casually over the armchair. Glancing back at the front door, she straightened up as quickly as she could. When her kids were little and she and Kevin had shared their big house out on West Springfield Drive, she'd kept it carefully neat and presentable. Even the few chaotic years she'd lived in the apartment with Janie and Jacob after the divorce, once Anna had gone out to school in Pittsburgh, she'd maintained an iron grip on her cleaning. But now that she lived alone, she had started letting things slide a bit. She didn't want to let Rana see that though. Her mother's voice chided her from somewhere in the back of her mind, reminding her that one couldn't invite guests into a messy home.

Footsteps creaked on the stairs, tentative as they reached the top, and then a soft knock rang through the living room. Marianne shoved the stack of magazines she held into a basket and kicked it under the coffee table and then called, "It's open!"

The door creaked slowly open, and Rana stepped inside. She'd hung her coat downstairs, left her boots, and closed the door behind her in socked feet. There was something strangely intimate about that—something domestic. Marianne liked it.

"Hi," she said, feeling a little silly.

"Hi," said Rana. "It's always strange to me that you live up here. Nice!" She hurried to clarify. "I can imagine the commute is quick. But sometimes if I'm working late, I hear footsteps upstairs and it's comforting to know it's you."

"I sometimes smell meat cooking and want to come down and visit," Marianne admitted. "Is that the same thing?"

Rana laughed. "I think it might be. You're always welcome." Her smile faded. "As long as I'm there, anyway."

"We'll figure it out," said Marianne. "Starting tomorrow, the real fight begins."

"Let's make sure you look good for it," said Rana. "Nour is usually my fashion consultant, but I think I can pass a little of her wisdom to you."

"Well then," said Marianne, pushing open her bedroom door and peeking inside to make sure her bed was made and there were no clothes on the floor—what was it about Rana that made her revert to about seventeen years old?—"I could use Nour's know-how for sure, whatever part of it you can share. And you always look nice," she added. "Your clothes, I mean. And the rest too." She closed her mouth before she could keep going.

Rana smiled. "Thank you. Well, I'll do my best." She followed Marianne in. "Your apartment is so lovely," she said. "It feels like a home."

Marianne shrugged. "We moved out for twenty years, but other than that, my family has lived here for a century. It's home, even when I don't live here. I've been meaning to update it, but I haven't had the time." She pulled open her closet, avoiding looking at the bed. "Thank you for helping," she said. "This isn't the kind of thing I'm good at." Out of the corner of her eye she saw Rana hovering, a little tense, by the door. She swallowed. "Feel free to make yourself comfortable," said Marianne. "Can I get you a drink or anything?"

"Oh, no thank you." Rana perched herself carefully on the very end of the bed. "I knew you'd lived here before, but I hadn't realized how much history was up here. Not just you, but your whole family."

"It's good and bad," Marianne replied, pulling out a suit and a long gray dress. "I used to think I wanted to leave it behind forever."

"Why?"

Marianne hooked the hangers over the top of the closet door and leaned against the head of the bed. "I don't know. I needed a change." She smiled. "And I got one, for a little while."

"With Kevin."

Marianne nodded. "We got married when we were nineteen. I'm glad we did—I love my children—but we were so young."

"Too young?"

"I'd been here in Swanley all my life. Everyone assumed I'd take over the shop. Dad's sisters had both moved across the country, and none of my cousins were interested. I think I felt trapped. I didn't want to be just out of high school and locked into a path for the rest of my life. Kevin seemed like a way out."

"You didn't want the bakery then?"

"It's complicated." Marianne gave a little laugh. "I'm sorry. I asked you up here to do me a favor, and here I am dumping my sad story all over you instead."

Rana reached across the expanse of quilt and rested a warm hand on Marianne's own. "That's all right," she said. "We're friends. Friends talk about their problems and their history."

Marianne glanced down at their hands, the dry warmth of Rana's featherlight on her own, Rana's skin brown against her olive-beige. Rana's fingers were longer than her own, her knuckles more delicate, but her fingertips were just as calloused from years with hot breads and meats as Marianne's. And they shared the lines and tiny scars of decades of hard work and good life.

"You're right," she said. "Friends do." She smiled up at Rana, tucking the tiny dream she'd had of being together in a different way deep down in her heart. "It's been so long since I made a new friend—one who didn't already know all my secrets—maybe I'd forgotten what it was like." Rana's friendship had come to mean so much to her. She didn't want to mess this up with her feelings. Besides, what if she woke up one day and the surprising attraction she felt toward the woman—something rare in her experience—was gone? Better not to risk it at all. Nobody got hurt if they were friends. Not Rana, and not even Marianne herself.

"You must have a few secrets," said Rana, patting her hand twice and then pulling away to stand and cast a critical eye on the two dangling outfits. "For instance, who in the world let you buy this dress?"

Marianne winced. "I thought it looked good back in 1997."

"Marianne, nothing that we thought looked good in 1997 looks good today." She tossed the hanger over the bed and put her hands on her hips, all business. "This blazer, though; this could work."

*

The day of the trial dawned clear and bright, the sun cutting through Marianne's window in a wide swath across her quilt and landing on the blouse and jacket combination Rana had hung on her closet doorknob.

The combination looked even better in the light than it had in the dimmer lamplight of the night before—a pale pink blouse, somewhere between rose and blush, with a jacket Anna had forgotten she'd stored in the closet years ago, a shade lighter than navy blue. The pants were gray and close-fitting, though not tight, and Marianne couldn't remember buying them, but they'd been in her closet forever.

It had been strangely intimate, showing Rana various combinations of clothing to try to pick the one that said *I'm a serious woman trying to save my business* without any tinge of too bright and too bold. She thought they'd struck a good balance, though, and it was funny, but knowing what she was going to wear took a bite out of the anxiety she'd been feeling about the first day of the case. Still, she was glad Rana would be in the courtroom today. They'd both closed their respective restaurants for the next two days—she didn't know how long the case would take, but she knew it wouldn't be over too quickly, not with Luke Leventi's tendency toward showboating. Besides, Rana had been winding down her hours, trying not to stock up on too many groceries now that she was a few weeks from the end of her lease.

Marianne tried not to see that as a vote of no confidence in her ability to win the case. It was pragmatic. And if she won, what then? If she got the whole building back, would Rana want to be her tenant? She didn't know the answer to that.

The silk of the blouse was cool and slick against her skin, armor going over her soft belly and breasts. With the jacket over it, the warm wool of the pants against her legs, and the nice boots she very rarely wore—Rana had asked about heels, and Marianne had admitted she'd been afraid to wear them since she'd sprained her ankle badly at Anna's high school graduation a decade ago—she felt like a different woman than the flour-smudged, comfortably cotton-clad person she normally was. This wasn't better, really, but—it was just exactly what she needed for the task at hand.

Kevin picked her up outside the bakery, his Jeep pulling up as she opened the door, and he actually whistled when she opened the door to climb in. "Wow," he said, looking her over. "You look good."

"Are you allowed to check out your ex-wife?" asked Marianne as he put the car back into drive.

He laughed. "I checked the divorce decree," he said. "Doesn't say I can't."

"Hmm," said Marianne, smiling. "That's an oversight, for sure."

He glanced at her as he slowed to a stop at the light at Oak and Main. "If it bothers you, though, I can stop making comments. Janie gave me a pretty thorough dressing-down about talking to women about how they look last time she called."

"It's all right," said Marianne, patting his elbow. "I'm glad she did, but I think we're in a place where we can talk this way."

Kevin smiled. "I think so too. I'm glad." He glanced at the sign on the left-hand side of the road. "Leaving Swanley," he said. "I hate doing that."

"I hate coming into Wilshire more," said Marianne. "Nothing good ever comes of this town."

He nodded his agreement as he pulled into the courthouse parking lot. "And you have to pay for the parking here too." He pulled out his wallet as he stepped down from the Jeep, sticking his card in the machine and pressing the button. "And the machine is broken. Great."

Marianne glanced around and spotted a sign fluttering on the old attendant's booth. "Pay inside, it says," she reported, shaking her head. "Wilshire."

"Wilshire," he agreed. "You ready?" He knocked on the booth and handed the attendant a card.

Marianne spotted a familiar group heading up the courthouse steps, Zeke supporting his great-grandfather as they climbed, Rana on his other side, splendid in a gray silk tunic with darker pants. "I'm ready," she said. "Let's get the bastard."

By the time they'd gotten to the steps and up to the door, Lila, Joe, Zeke, and Rana were just entering the courthouse. Zeke looked Marianne over, eyebrows raised. "Looking good, boss," he commented, and Joe elbowed him. "Eyes to yourself, boy. She's more woman than you could handle."

Marianne wasn't sure whether to be flattered or offended. Rana was smiling, just a little, when Marianne risked a glance her way. She seemed to be fighting it. Kevin had no such debate, as he was chortling into a fist. Zeke, on the other hand, was flushing deep brown.

"I wasn't—" He stopped. "I didn't—"

She reached out and patted his cheek. "I'm almost old enough to be your grandmother, kiddo," she said kindly. "Don't worry, I didn't think you were being creepy."

He glared at Joe. "See?"

Joe grinned, showing the gaps in his teeth.

"It's that time, folks," said Lila.

"Lead the way, Counselor," replied Marianne and followed her into the courthouse.

Lila knew her way around, and Marianne was grateful. Lila led them right to the security station, which sat around a corner and behind a cluster of potted plants Marianne suspected were both older than she was and also fake. The ceiling was uncomfortably high, the Brutalist architecture leading to strange angles and proportions and a preponderance of cement and gunmetal-gray carpeting. It wasn't a building made to induce a feeling of comfort in visitors. But then, unless they were getting married or naturalized, there were not many comfortable reasons to be in a courthouse. She was suddenly grateful for the unintended architectural education she'd gotten over the years from Anna.

Security walked her through the metal detector, Joe grumbling at having to put his cane on the conveyor for the X-ray machine and walk through without it. Zeke helped him, holding his arm carefully and walking at his great-grandfather's speed. Marianne, setting her own watch and purse on the conveyor, glanced at him and smiled. A good kid. Rana handed Joe his cane as it cleared the X-ray machine.

The receptionist directed them down the hallway to an imposing set of double doors, oak and stained dark, and the group paused in front of them.

"This is it," said Lila. "I'm willing to bet Luke Leventi is already inside. Marianne and I will be at the counsel's table while the rest of you will be in the gallery. Marianne, only speak if the judge speaks to you, all right? And call them Your Honor at all times."

"Got it," said Marianne, nodding. "Okay."

"Let's do this," said Zeke. "Let's squash the motherfucker."

"Ezekiel!" chided Joe.

"Sorry, Grandpa. Let's squash the, uh, dipshit?"

Joe gave him a warning glance but didn't comment.

Chapter Nineteen

The judge—Judge Marsha Petit—wasn't someone Lila had worked with before, which made Lila and Kevin both a little nervous. As they settled at the defendant's table, the rest of their crowd behind the divider, Marianne tried not to look over at Luke Leventi on the other side of the courtroom.

"Mr. Leventi," said the judge, "I understand we're here to discuss a will you're challenging."

"That's correct, Your Honor." Luke flipped open a folder. Marianne, leaning forward, recognized a photocopy of the will, her father's handwriting familiar even from a dozen feet away.

"And this will was filed—" the judge paused, glancing down at her file. "This will was filed last week. A day after your challenge was recorded." She looked up. "You're an overachiever, Mr. Leventi."

He smiled, white teeth glinting as he turned on his charm. "I try to be, Your Honor."

"Well." She leaned back. "What evidence do you have to contradict the will as filed?"

"Where's his lawyer?" Marianne asked Lila quietly, leaning close as Luke began to speak.

"He's representing himself," she murmured back. "It wouldn't be my choice. Not usually a great idea."

"He thinks he's the best lawyer in the county, I'll bet," said Marianne. "I guess he didn't think he could find someone better."

"I'm better," said Lila. "Don't worry." She patted Marianne's hand. "Objection," she said, loudly, interrupting Luke. "There's no statute of limitations on filing a will. Not if it's newly discovered."

"Ms. Shapiro has a point," said Judge Petit. "Mr. Leventi, the fact that fifty years have passed doesn't mean anything about the will's validity."

"I'm aware of the law," said Luke, a little snippy. "But the witnesses are no longer living and therefore cannot confirm their witnessing of the signing. We have no idea if those signatures are valid."

"I have copies of Mr. Liu's wife's death certificate," said Lila. "He signed it in 1985. And here—" she pulled out a second sheet, "—I have a copy of his honorable discharge, from 1970, with another nearly identical signature."

"Bring those to the bench, please," said the judge. Lila did, and Luke hurried up beside her. The judge considered the pages, holding them up to the light next to the page of her copy of the will. Marianne wished she could see the pages more closely—it seemed to be taking her an awfully long time to check them over.

Finally, Judge Petit handed both pages back to Lila. "They seem to match," she said. "And Mr. Asmir?"

Lila shook her head. "We weren't able to find any records of his, Your Honor."

"Two witnesses are needed for a legal will," said Luke. "If one's identity can't be verified—"

"You can't disprove his identity, can you, Mr. Leventi?"

Marianne could see a muscle in his jaw jumping, all the way from her seat. "No, Your Honor."

"Then let's move on from this. The witnesses stand."

Luke flipped to another page. "Even if the will was, in fact, written by Mr. Windmere in 1969, I have records from that period which bring his mental competence into question."

"Medical records are private," objected Lila. "I have to object to that, Your Honor."

"Not if they're notes on a legal matter," responded Luke.

"What's he talking about?" Marianne whispered to Lila.

"I'm not sure yet," Lila admitted.

A *tap-tapping* fingernails-on-wood sound behind her made Marianne turn in her seat. Kevin was leaning up to the railing, and she bent closer.

"That fourth of July," he whispered. "I think that's where he's going with this."

"Oh, my god," said Marianne. "You're right."

"I have the transcript here of a police interview with Mr. Windmere in July of 1970," Luke was saying. "He admitted to hallucinating gunshots and attacking a man walking by his storefront."

"That's not what happened!" Marianne said, forgetting the instructions not to speak. "The guy surprised a veteran in the middle of a fireworks display. He was fine!"

"Ms. Windmere," said the judge sternly. "Please refrain from interrupting the plaintiff."

Marianne slowly sat, face hot, as Luke turned a small smile her direction. She didn't meet his eyes.

"As I was saying, Your Honor, Daniel Windmere was not in a sound state of mind in 1969."

"What's your evidence of that?" Judge Petit narrowed her eyes. "Many veterans struggle with some form of posttraumatic stress disorder, Mr. Leventi. I'm going to need more than one fireworks-related outburst to prove him non compos mentis."

Luke shuffled his papers. "He spent a night at Medfield State Hospital in 1970, after his wife reported him a danger to himself."

Marianne closed her eyes. She remembered that night as clearly as if it were last month, not fifty years ago. And she knew Luke remembered it too. His father had been there, arguing with her father, taking his gun from him. Luke had been there, hiding with her in her room. Her dad had come back from Vietnam scared and angry, and she remembered Luke—a few years younger than her, not more than seven or so at the time—had asked her if their dads were going to hurt each other. She'd assured him they weren't even though she wasn't sure herself. She opened her eyes and stared at the man that scared little boy had grown into.

"You have proof of that, I assume?"

"I was present when he was taken there," Luke said. He didn't look at Marianne this time.

The judge sighed. "Do you have a date?"

"August 28th," he said promptly.

"So nearly a year after the will was written and witnessed."

Luke didn't respond.

"Mr. Leventi, you're grasping at straws. Unless you have anything more substantial, I'm going to have to declare the will valid." Judge Petit waited a moment, and when Luke didn't answer, she stamped the page. "I can't see any merit in the challenge." She glanced up at the clock and frowned. "Now, is that all the business here today?"

"No, Your Honor." Luke stood, clearing his throat. "I would like to file a claim of Adverse Possession on 121 Main Street, suite B, on the grounds that Ms. Windmere neglected to take possession of the property while my tenants and I occupied it openly and hostilely from 1990 to 2010. And I have witnesses."

"That's a serious charge, Mr. Leventi."

Lila pushed herself upright. "Objection. We were not informed of any witnesses today."

The judge sighed, "Mr. Leventi, are you adding additional witnesses to the docket today?"

"I am not, Your Honor."

"Then, Ms. Shapiro, let's let Mr. Leventi continue and see where he's going with this."

Lila sat back down. Marianne's stomach did a nervous flip. Behind her, she heard fabric rustle and the low tones of Rana and Kevin's voices whispering.

"As I was saying," said Luke, "Ms. Windmere showed no interest in claiming the property at suite B. I merely decided not to let the place fall into disrepair when it could be used since Ms. Windmere ignored her responsibility to the building."

"Objection," said Lila again.

"Keep it to the facts, Mr. Leventi. Speculation doesn't help your case."

Marianne thought that may be less than true. She should have done more research; she told herself again. How could she have assumed everything was fine? Maybe Luke was right. Maybe she didn't deserve the building.

A hand patted her shoulder, and she turned to see Rana leaning over the rail. "What?" she asked, resisting the urge to cover the hand with her own.

"We all know he's lying," Rana whispered. "Just...if you were wondering."

Marianne felt a slow smile spread over her face. "Thanks," she whispered back.

"Besides," Lila was continuing. "Ms. Windmere was not aware of her ownership of the property."

"That's not relevant," protested Luke.

"Are you a judge, Mr. Leventi?" asked Judge Petit. She paused. "Let the record reflect that Mr. Leventi is shaking his head, please."

Luke glowered.

"Back to the question at hand." Judge Petit lowered her glasses to peer at Marianne over them. "Ms. Windmere, is this true? Did you not enter the property for over twenty years?"

"Don't answer that," said Kevin quietly. "Let your lawyer answer."

Lila stood. "My client can't say whether or not she entered the premises of 121B during that time, Your Honor. She doesn't typically record her every moment for posterity." She turned toward the other table. "Does the plaintiff have any proof she did not?"

"That's a good question," said the Judge. "Well, Mr. Leventi?"

Luke stood. Gathering a folder, he brought it up to the bench. Lila stood and took the second folder he passed through the bailiff.

He smiled, and the sudden moment of glee faded as quickly as it had arrived. "I do, Your Honor." He opened a folder, revealing a thick stack of papers. "I have notarized statements from each tenant in the period under discussion, swearing that Ms. Windmere did not enter their storefronts during their tenures."

"May we have a brief recess to consider this new information?" asked Lila. "My client and I need to review these statements."

"Ten minutes, Ms. Shapiro," said the judge.

"Thank you, Your Honor," said Lila, and flipped open the folder, twisting to face Marianne. "What do you think? Are these true?"

"I don't understand what's happening," Marianne confessed, anxiety roiling in her stomach. "What does he need to know that for?"

Lila sighed and ran a hand through her long, curly hair before twisting it back up and pinning it with a clip. "Adverse possession. It's a stupid, leftover law from before the days of computerized records. It means if somebody squats somewhere for long enough, they can take ownership of it legally."

"What? That doesn't make sense! You're saying because I didn't know I owned it, I might lose it?"

"That's exactly what I'm saying." She shook her head. "I'm sorry, Marianne. I had no idea he was planning this. We're going to have to play it by ear, okay?"

Marianne swallowed hard, glancing back at their friends, watching worriedly from the gallery. Kevin leaned forward. "He's trying a hell of a hard sell," he reassured her. "And even if we lose, he just gets to keep the part of the building we already believed he owned." He smiled faintly. "And I have to admit, you've got a great lawyer."

"He's not going to win," said Zeke, and Rana and Joe nodded. "It's your damn building, boss."

Lila closed the folder. "All right," she said. "Time's up." She looked at Marianne and then at Rana behind them. "We're going to do our best, okay?"

Judge Petit rapped her gavel. "Folks, let's get back to business. Ms. Shapiro, have you and your client reviewed the documents?"

Lila stood. "We have, Your Honor."

"And have you reached any conclusions?"

Kevin leaned over the rail, whispering, "She's getting fed up with this trial."

Marianne ignored him.

"We agree on the possibility that Ms. Windmere did not enter the property but contest the claim of adverse possession on other grounds."

"What grounds are those, Ms. Shapiro?" The judge crossed her arms.

"The will we've just established is valid, Your Honor." Lila picked up the document. "Mr. Windmere states that Mr. Leventi's father is to be granted conservatorship over the entire property, including the space now known as suite B. By authorizing this, he states an implicit invitation to Simon Leventi and his heirs to enter both properties. Any invitation, as Mr. Leventi surely knows, invalidates any claim of adverse possession."

"Interesting. Mr. Leventi? Rebuttal?"

Luke stood. "I am not my father," he said. "While my father may have been issued an invitation, I was not. When both my father and Daniel Windmere passed away, the invitation implied in the will was rendered no longer relevant."

"But your sworn statements cover the period from 1990 to 2010," said Lila. "Your father ran the business you claim as your own for part of that time, and it does not include the last nine years." She turned to the judge. "I move to remove the statements covering the period from 1990 to 1994 from the evidence."

"That seems in line with what Mr. Leventi is claiming. The statements from Mr. Phan, Mr. Carlisle, and Ms. L'Esperance are out."

"That still leaves all these years of sworn statements, under my tenure," said Luke.

"Ms. Windmere has entered the property recently," said Lila. "In the last six months, she has entered suite *B* nine times."

"You have proof of this?" asked the judge.

"Ms. Rana Wahbi, the proprietor of the Cairo Grill, will swear to it, as can numerous other customers of both establishments."

"Ms. Shapiro did not furnish a list of witnesses to this," said Luke, crossing his arms.

"Ms. Shapiro was not informed you were going to be opening what is essentially a whole new suit," chided the judge. "As you are well aware. I'll allow the witness." She looked back to Lila. "Will you need time to find this witness?"

"She's in the courtroom already," said Lila. She turned and whispered something to Rana, who had gone a little pale, but who nodded. "And she's willing to testify to that effect."

"Well, we're in luck. Any objection to Ms. Wahbi testifying, Mr. Leventi?"

"Yes," said Luke. "Ms. Wahbi is known to be romantically involved with Ms. Windmere, rendering any testimony she may give questionable."

"That's why we swear people in, Mr. Leventi. Trust the process."

"Ms. Wahbi isn't a Christian," said Luke. "You can't swear a Muslim in on a Bible."

"Luckily, in this country we have a division of church and state." Judge Petit said, reaching under her desk. "Ms. Wahbi, do you have a preference? We have a number of Qurans available. As well as Torahs, Gitas, and the Constitution."

Rana stood and cleared her throat. "No preference, Your Honor. Any Quran will do."

"And will you be prejudiced toward Ms. Windmere, or will you tell the truth once sworn in?"

"I try to always tell the truth, Your Honor, sworn in or not. But today I will swear to it, yes," said Rana, and someone behind Marianne—she suspected Zeke—muffled a snort.

"As we all should be truthful in all our dealings. Please come to the witness stand, Ms. Wahbi. Thank you."

As Rana was sworn in, Marianne tried to calm her racing heart. Luke thought she and Rana were romantically involved? What did Rana think of that? Marianne knew rumors had been swirling about them—it wasn't so big of a town, after all—but to have it stated so openly and boldly was a little shocking. This was New England. She had assumed Luke knew you weren't supposed to talk about these things in public. Besides, it wasn't true. It might have been briefly, but now? Now she didn't know where they stood.

Rana settled into the witness stand, and Lila walked over to her. "Ms. Wahbi, has Ms. Windmere been to the Cairo Grill?"

Rana smiled and glanced at Marianne, the pallor fading from her cheeks and replaced with a deeper tint. "Yes. She has. She's eaten many meals in the past few months."

"And you and she are socially acquainted beyond the bounds of neighbors, are you not?"

"We are," said Rana.

"How long have you been friendly?"

"Since November," Rana replied. "Well, we've been neighbors longer, but that's how long we've been friends."

Warmth sparked in Marianne's chest at the comment.

"And you frequently dine together, either in your restaurant or in Ms. Windmere's property?"

"We do."

"No further questions," said Lila.

"Mr. Leventi, your witness," said Judge Petit.

Luke stood. "Ms. Wahbi, is it true you've run the Cairo Grill for six months in 121 Main Street, Suite B?"

"Yes," said Rana. "I had hoped to run it for longer, but I've been told my lease will not be renewed."

"That's unfortunate," said Luke.

"I wish you'd thought that before sending me the letter that terminated my lease," replied Rana.

"Stick to answering the questions, Ms. Wahbi," said the judge.

"I'm sorry, Your Honor. Yes. Six months."

"And in the six months, isn't it true you became romantically entangled with Ms. Windmere, your neighbor and the defendant in this case?"

Rana hesitated, glancing at Marianne again, who felt her face turning a deep shade of pink. "We're close friends," said Rana.

"And lovers?"

Rana opened her mouth to reply just as Lila said, "Objection!"

Rana closed her mouth, and Marianne relaxed a bit, heart thudding. She both wanted to know how Rana had been about to answer and didn't want to know. Schroedinger's romantic declaration.

"You've already ruled their relationship, whatever form it takes, isn't relevant to this trial."

"Sustained. Mr. Leventi, wrap it up."

A muscle twitched in Luke's jaw as he ground his teeth. "No further questions, Your Honor."

"All right. Ms. Wahbi, you're done. Thank you."

Rana walked back to the gate and settled beside Zeke and Joe, avoiding Marianne's eyes. Marianne swallowed hard.

"I'd like to call Marianne Windmere to the stand," said Luke.

The judge frowned. "I suppose you can do that," she said. "Ms. Windmere, please come up to the front. What would you like to be sworn in on? A Bible? The Constitution? As I wasn't notified of your being called, I wasn't able to research your particular belief system."

"The Constitution will be fine," said Marianne. "Thank you."

The chair in the witness stand was still a little warm, and Marianne didn't care if it was a little weird to take comfort from Rana's residual heat.

"Now, Ms. Windmere, your father passed away in 1982; is that correct?"

"You know it is. Yes."

"And you refused to take control of his business? You were too busy?"

"I left it in your father's hands—yes—to maintain while I finished school and had my first two children."

"But you had stated no interest in taking over the business, is that correct?"

"No. I always knew I would take it over someday."

"But you didn't want to?"

Marianne hesitated. "I was not as excited about it as I could have been," she said carefully.

"And isn't it true you were relieved when Simon Leventi took over the day-to-day running of the business while sending you most of the profits?"

"I was grateful to your father—yes—before I knew he had lied about parts of the business."

"What parts were those?"

"He lowered the quality of some of our goods, using inferior ingredients, and laid off a number of longtime staff in favor of newer employees."

"But you didn't visit or look closely at the records?"

"I did when I realized the business was in danger of failing."

"But suite *B* was never a concern of yours?"

"It was once I came home and found our business had been cut in half, and there were strangers in our building."

"But you never looked into the sale."

"Not until now. I was busy recovering the business from neglect."

"And when you removed my father from control over your business, did your profits improve?"

"Not right away. I had to rehire my old staff and rebuild our reputation with less space and equipment while raising three children. What was your father doing in suite B? Didn't the first three businesses he tried to put in there fail?"

"Well, yes, but—" Luke hedged.

"And didn't my business win Swanley Business Council's Business of the Year Award four years after nearly closing down?"

"It did—"

Marianne leaned forward. "And didn't your father nearly drive my business into the ground and then buy part of it to try to recover some of the profits by becoming a slumlord?"

"That's not true! When my father bought the property—" Luke's face had reddened, and his mouth slammed closed. He swallowed. "I misspoke. When my father took possession of the property, he improved the location substantially, both through renovation and good management."

"Mr. Leventi." The judge slid her glasses off, letting them dangle around her neck. "This is an interesting development. It would appear to me that you didn't misspeak."

"Your Honor?"

She crossed her arms. "Tonya, would you read back the transcript?"

The stenographer cleared her throat. Marianne glanced over at her, surprised—she hadn't noticed the woman there, typing away. "Mr. Leventi: That's not true. When my father bought the property. Pause. I misspoke. When my father took possession of the property."

"Thank you, Tonya." The judge turned back to Luke. "You believed he bought the property."

Luke sat in silence, eyes darting around the courtroom. Kevin leaned forward over the rail and whispered gleefully, loudly enough for Marianne to hear from the stand, "I bet he's regretting self-representing now!"

Lila shushed him, eyes intent on Luke.

"Mr. Leventi?" Judge Petit prompted.

He cleared his throat again. "I said I misspoke. I was confused by all the rhetoric."

"Ms. Windmere, you may return to your seat." Marianne stepped down and hurried to the table, dropping into her seat beside Lila. Her heart pounded a staccato beat in her chest, her hands trembling. She'd turned the tables on him, beaten him at his own game, and she should feel thrilled, but what she felt instead was more like a terror hangover after a nighttime scare.

The judge smiled. "I think I can rule on the adverse possession charge you've just brought up, Mr. Leventi. Denied. You had no idea you were illegally occupying a property that you did not own. And as for the will?" She turned to Marianne and Lila. "Ms. Windmere, this will clearly shows your father intended you to have the property, and I'm inclined to believe you're entitled to the entire building unless Mr. Leventi can produce a record of sale? Or has my rhetoric confused you?" She turned toward Luke and waited for him to respond. He stayed silent.

Behind Marianne, she heard both Zeke and Joe smother snorts. She took another deep breath, feeling the panic recede. She was safe here. She was safe, and she was *winning*.

Judge Petit banged her gavel once. "In the case of Leventi vs. Windmere, I rule that the will in question is valid. Furthermore, I rule that due to Mr. Leventi's inability to prove either his ownership of suite *B* or his hostile and open occupation of it, the deed reverts to the original owner and possessor of the original deed—or in this case, his heir." She stood. "Adjourned."

There was a long moment of silence as she picked up her novel and her folder and disappeared out the back door.

"That's it? We won?" Marianne turned in her seat to stare at Rana, who had both hands over her mouth. "Oh my god! We won!"

Kevin leaned forward over the rail to clap Marianne on the shoulder. "You did," he said, shaking Lila's hand with his free one. "Congratulations!"

Across the courtroom, Luke Leventi sat beside his assistant, whispering fiercely. They were so wrapped up in their discussion, pointing fingers and flipping through notes, that they didn't notice the state trooper calling someone on his radio and then nodding, hanging up, and starting toward the Leventi side of the courtroom. But Marianne did, and she and Rana exchanged a look.

"Lucas Leventi?" said the officer, stopping in front of the table. "Come with me, please."

"I'm speaking with my lawyer," said Leventi. "Can it wait?"

"We can do this the easy way," said the officer, a slight smile on his face, and that's when Marianne recognized him. "Or we can do this down at the station."

One of the many businesses that had been a short-term tenant at what was now Rana's shop had been a gourmet pasta shop, run by a high school classmate of Marianne's. That had been back in the mideighties, but the girl's older brother, Joey, looked exactly the same—just a little wider and a little less hair—as he had when he graduated in 1977, two years ahead of Marianne. He might not have been waiting forty years to arrest Leventi, specifically, but he was certainly enjoying the opportunity to take in the man who had ruined his little sister's dreams of culinary stardom.

Kevin leaned forward, voice low. "Tax evasion."

Marianne and Rana both turned. "What?" asked Marianne.

"I got a text from Gerry over in the sheriff's office, who heard it from his cousin at the state police. That's what they're getting him on."

"He's getting arrested?" Rana craned her neck to see the other table. "I don't know how I feel about that."

"You should feel good," said Zeke. "Definitely. I do."

"He hasn't paid income taxes, at least to the state, on any of the rent anyone has paid him since he started renting 121B out," explained Kevin. "Neither did his father. Luke has paid property tax ever since he took over the business, and I'll bet he tries to argue that can be used to pay his debt now that he's definitely not the owner, but I doubt they'll buy that excuse."

"Why would he pay taxes on it?" asked Zeke. "He knew he didn't own the place."

Marianne grinned. "I know the answer to this one." She turned in her seat as Luke Leventi disappeared through the back door of the courtroom. "He's been trying to take my building, all the way back then. This was part of the gamble. It was a long con."

"How does that work?"

Joe answered. "If you don't own a place, but nobody's using it, you can live on it and pay its taxes and eventually it's yours." He shook his head. "That law hasn't worked out so well for Black folks, generally, or for other people of color, let me tell you." His lips turned up in a smile. "And it's not working out for him much better."

"What're you going to do now?" asked Kevin. "You've gotten your building back. What happens next?"

Marianne smiled. "We go home. We get our sign. We run good restaurants."

Rana smiled, as well, but it didn't reach her eyes. "We have to talk about my lease too."

"Later," Marianne assured her. "For now, we're celebrating. And consider this month's rent paid. We can talk later." She stood. "I say we go out and celebrate. Drinks on me at the Lazy Dog!" She pointed to the door, and the group filed out, accepting handshakes and congratulations from the crowd in the gallery.

"I'll see you tomorrow," said Rana as they stepped out. "I don't drink, remember?"

Marianne laughed. "I forgot, sorry. How about this? I'll buy you a soda and a blooming onion."

"Come on," said Zeke, slinging an arm around Rana's shoulders. "I can't drink, either, but I'm going to eat so many jalapeno poppers Marianne's going to regret offering to pay."

Rana's mouth curled into a smile that her lips fought a losing battle against. "Fine," she said. "But I'm going to eat some of those jalapeno poppers too."

Zeke cheered, and the group piled out onto the street and down the road toward the Lazy Dog.

Chapter Twenty

Doris slapped Zeke on the shoulder, making him spray virgin piña colada all over himself and blush dark brown. "You guys did it," she said gleefully. "You took that bastard down!"

"I never realized you hated the man so much," said Marianne. "I mean, he's awful, but you seem a little more pissed off than most."

"Hah!" Doris took a long slug of her beer and handed Zeke a napkin. "He evicted my baby sister!"

"What?"

"My kid sister, Tabitha. She lived out in that new block of apartments he built on Greendale back in the late nineties. You know the ones."

Marianne did—they looked beautiful from the outside, but apparently were filled with hazards and shoddy workmanship. She nodded.

"Well, her best friend broke up with her boyfriend— long story, but it was a bad situation—and she moved in with Tabby for a couple weeks until she could find her own place. Problem was, apparently her lease said she'd be the only occupant. I guess somebody said something to Luke, and next thing I knew, they were *both* crashing in my basement." She shook her head. "Imagine kicking someone out because they helped a friend."

"I don't have to imagine it," said Rana. "He nearly did the same to me."

Doris smiled, reaching out to put her hand on Rana's wrist. "I'm glad you're not getting kicked out," she said. "Even if I do crave a Coolatta once in a while."

Zeke groaned. "Those things are disgusting. I'll make you an iced latte that'll blow your mind."

"Hey," said Kevin, pointing at the television in the corner. "Check it out." He leaned over the bar, asking the bartender to turn the volume up. "They're talking about the case."

Jesse Laurence sat behind his desk at Channel 13, looking stern. "And in local news, get ready for another special election in the towns of Wilshire, Swanley, and Greensborough next month. Karen has the report from Wilshire Courthouse."

"Thanks, Jesse. Well, I'm standing outside Wilshire County Courthouse, hours after a court case against incoming Representative Lucas Leventi of the Wilshire Second District. You may recall he won the primary last month in a surprise upset after former Representative Joshua Robertson was appointed Commissioner of Public Health by the Governor. Everyone had assumed that as he was running unopposed in the general election, he'd be taking the seat by default. Now things don't look like they'll be that simple when Wilshire heads to the polls again in May, because as soon as the case was decided, the state police took him into custody on charges of tax evasion. Whether Ms. Hechevarria will be running again as an Independent, or whether another candidate will appear in the next few weeks, today's events will certainly add spice to a race everyone assumed was decided. And while Representative Leventi is, of course, innocent until proven guilty, our sources confirm two things for us: one, campaigns run from behind bars don't generally end well, and two, the evidence against Representative Leventi is very compelling. For WBSC, I'm Karen Gilcrest."

"May?" Zeke grinned widely. "Hey, I'll be able to vote in that one!"

Marianne hugged him around the shoulders, laughing. "That's something to celebrate."

"Maybe I'll run," mused Kevin. "What do you think?"

"I think you'd hate it," said Marianne, frankly.

Kevin smiled. "You're probably right."

"If you're bored, I'm sure there're volunteers needed at the Hechevarria campaign," said Doris. "It'd be a shame if he won just because he made it on the ballot."

Looking thoughtful, Kevin pulled out his phone. "You know, I've got Linda Tyler's number in here somewhere. I bet she could get me in touch with them." With that, he disappeared.

"Nice dodge, boss," said Zeke. "He'll be running his whole term out of the bakery if you let him run."

"I don't let that man do anything. Not my job anymore." Marianne raised her glass and clinked it on Zeke's soda. "To the bakery."

"I'll drink to that," said Doris, raising her own bottle. "Let's celebrate."

*

Things had finally settled down at the bakery, the crowds of well-wishers finally thinning into the usual regular customers and the occasional tourist. Marianne was glad of it—the extra business had been nice, as had seeing old neighbors she hadn't spoken to in years, but she and Zeke could only handle so much. And she really didn't want to hire anyone new. She'd never been a news story before, and she didn't want to be one now.

There was still the question of suite *B*—Rana's restaurant was closed, for now, awaiting the official survey and the new negotiation of leasing, if she wanted to stay at all. Marianne wasn't looking forward to that conversation. The friendship they'd built, the tentative first flutters of something more; she wasn't sure how well they'd do once she was Rana's landlord. But then, she didn't want to lose her either. What would it be like to go next door and have a stranger there? Would that be worse than having to ask Rana for rent every month? Was it even legal to have a crush on your tenant? She didn't know.

What she did know was that Ray Bell was stopping by with what he said was a very nice surprise for her this morning, and she could hear him honking the horn of his big parks truck on the street. When she poked her head out the door, he pointed around behind the building and grinned at her from the drivers' seat. In the back window of his truck she spotted his German Shepherd, Molly, trying to stick her head out the open sliver. She waved back at Ray, confirming she'd seen him through the open door and handed her tongs to Zeke. "Watch things a few minutes, all right?"

Zeke nodded, without looking up from his Kindle, but Marianne knew that if someone walked in, he'd have the sense to head back to the counter. Probably. Depended how good the book was.

She cut through the kitchen and out the back door as Ray pulled into the lot, parking his big city maintenance truck in front of four parked cars. "It's here," he said, pulling a drill from his toolbox and a measuring tape from his pocket. "Let me get the screws set up, and we'll hang it." He pointed to a large rectangle wrapped in tarp in the bed of the truck. "Take a look."

Marianne pulled the tarp back and gasped. She hadn't expected the sign to look so nice. The letters were sharp, clean black capitals, at least three inches high, and it read, "Three hour parking for customers of 121 Main Street." In smaller letters below, it continued: "All others will be towed, by order of Swanley City Council." To get the sign that had been the reason for the whole process and the result felt anticlimactic. Now she had so much more than a parking lot. She had her family's building, all of it, back under one name.

Ray hefted the sign, pulling it free of the tarp and carrying it to the wall. A few steps up a ladder and six screws later, the sign hung proudly over their little lot. "It's a good thing you found that will," he said. "Otherwise, this wouldn't have happened. Not ever. You'd be staring at the back of a donut shop and wondering why you had no customers."

"It wasn't me who found the will," said Marianne. "Zeke Mitchell did; you know that."

"It's folks like you two who are the backbone of this town, you know," said Ray. "Your dad and grandad and your line and his too—all the way back—have been keeping us fed and happy here. Guardian angels!"

Marianne laughed. "Ray, you take better care of me than I ever have of you. And besides, without Rana, this wouldn't have been possible either. You don't have to be born in this town to love it." She raised an eyebrow. "There are plenty of Leventis on the town charter, and you see how much good he's done the place."

Ray gave the sign one last tug to make sure it hung securely and then shrugged. "Well, you might be right. Glad we got this back in the family, anyway."

"Oh, you know we're all related to the Leventis somewhere down the line. Small town, white people, we've got to be."

"I'm kicking him out of the family then. He ain't welcome any longer at the reunions." Ray laughed. "I'll see you around, Marianne."

She bid him goodbye and stood a few more minutes, looking at the building her great-grandfather had built on his father's dream. Windmere was an institution in town, one of the few businesses nearly as old as the town itself, and she thought she might have forgotten what that meant for a while. She'd been too wrapped up in the moment-to-moment life of the bakery rather than the long view. But May Day was coming up in a few months, and looking out at the newly paved, painted parking lot and the small park beyond, she thought maybe it was time to resurrect some of her grandfather's old traditions.

The Cairo Grill's back door swung open, Rana appearing in the sunlight. She smiled at Marianne, coming to stand beside her, looking up at the sign. "We did it," she said. "We got those people out of the lot."

"It took a little more work than I thought it would," admitted Marianne.

"It was worth it," said Rana decisively. "We did a good thing, Marianne." She nodded, patting Marianne on the shoulder. "I'm cleaning out my oven, but if you'll be open later, I may come by for a coffee, if that's all right?"

Marianne smiled. "You're always welcome, Rana."

Rana's smile widened, showing white teeth. "Well, thank you, neighbor." She gave the sign one more approving look and then pulled her shawl tighter around her shoulders and made her way back into her restaurant. Marianne watched her go, a lightness blossoming in her chest. Could it all really work out?

Joe was sitting with his great-grandson when Marianne got back inside, and he gave her a warm smile. "I ran into Ray Bell out there in the lot," he said. "He said that lot's officially all yours now, and the whole building besides. Sounds like a good reason for a celebration."

"He's just angling to get you to make apple pie out of season," said Zeke, and Joe pointed at him, shaking his head.

"Make it an early strawberry pie, and you've got yourself a deal."

Zeke and Joe both stared at her. "What deal?" Joe finally asked suspiciously.

"I'm bringing back the May Day festival, if I can," she said. "Free pie for everyone. And, hopefully, other things from our neighbors too." She smiled. "We've got our town back. We need to celebrate."

Joe let out a cackle that startled both Marianne and Zeke. "You did well, Marianne. Your great-granddad would be proud of you." He shook his head. "All those people thought they were the only ones Simon and Lucas were getting to. Should have gotten them to talk to each other earlier."

"I didn't know," said Marianne. "None of us did. That's how they got us all."

"I hope he enjoys his cell," said Zeke vehemently. "I hope he has one of those toilets in the middle of the room and a cellmate who says really creepy things to him in the dark."

Marianne and Joe both turned to Zeke, whose skin blushed a shade darker than usual. "What?"

"That was very specific, boy," said Joe.

"I watch a lot of prison shows," Zeke muttered. "Sue me. And you can't say you wouldn't hate that if you were in there."

"He's got a point," said Marianne after a long pause. She cleared her throat, changing the subject. "Anyway. I hope you're both ready to cancel any May Day plans you might have had."

"Is Rana going to make her haw—her hasa—her meat dumpling things?" asked Zeke, stumbling over the word.

"Hawawshi, and yes," replied Marianne. "And I'm going to talk to the other restaurants in town, and maybe Gretel over at the toy store to see if there's something she can do for the kids."

"I think the old maypole is still around somewhere," said Joe. "If I recall, we last used it in, oh, '73? Or, '74? The ribbons might be dust, but the pole was good strong wood, and I'm sure it's just moldering in the back of city hall somewhere."

"Can you find out?" asked Marianne. "That would be amazing to have that piece of history with us."

"We haven't had a May Day festival since the seventies," said Joe. "I think maybe the town needs a way to celebrate."

Chapter Twenty-One

The final shimmer of sunshine disappeared behind the steeple of the Congregational Church on Chestnut Street as Marianne stumbled out of the crowd of dancers to drop onto a bench at the edge of the green. The bonfire burned bright across the park, and in the center stood the maypole woven with dozens of ribbons of every color, the same one she'd danced around every spring of her childhood. Above, the stars dazzled, a sliver of moon barely visible above city hall to the west. Marianne breathed in the woodsmoke and laughter and let a smile steal across her lips.

This was her town, the town she'd fled only to come right back, and she loved it deep in her bones. She could leave, but she'd always find her way there again in the end. Swanley was in her blood, in the flour ground under her nails, in the bright smiles of kids whose grandparents she'd known for half a century. And it was in the new people, too, the ones who'd found this little, beautiful, strange town and fought their way into its soul.

Rana slid from the crowd and sank onto the bench beside her, tilting her head back to watch the sky with Marianne.

Marianne tried not to stare at her, at her thick black hair shining in the moonlight, at her sparkling eyes, at the flush on her cheeks. She hadn't seen Rana much since the trial, too busy with figuring out the old accounts and finally organizing all the files her grandfather and father had apparently never put in order. She'd also been to city hall to make sure the new survey would be conducted soon—she didn't want any confusion about her property ever again. But she had been starting to wonder if Rana was avoiding her. She was glad for this evidence to the contrary.

"Beautiful night," Rana said quietly, breathing a little hard. "I danced with Ray's granddaughter and Zeke's nieces for an hour."

"People are happy," said Marianne. "It's because of you."

Rana turned back to her. "Me? You're the one who figured it out."

"No, I'm not. You put the pieces together. You had to risk everything when Leventi tried to kick you out. You could have left, but you didn't. You stayed and realized something was wrong. If you hadn't come to Swanley, we wouldn't be celebrating tonight." Marianne reached out and put her hand on Rana's, a little shiver of excitement fluttering through her. "You're the reason for all of this."

Rana turned her hand upward, fingers lacing with Marianne's. "Thank you," she whispered. "For this night. And everything else."

Marianne squeezed her hand, watching Zeke lift one of his sister's kids high in the air, laughing. His face was open and delighted, a mirror to the little girl in his arms, and her heart ached for him just the slightest. At least the door was opening, if slightly, to the possibility of reconciliation. His sisters were on his side now. He and Joe had had them over at the shop, when they came into town to show their kids the May Day they'd grown up with, and they'd had a long talk about Zeke and about the family. They apparently hadn't realized how bad it was with his parents. They'd thought it was his choice to move out. But now they knew, so he had them. And he had Joe, of course—but Joe was turning ninety-nine soon. Joe wouldn't be around forever. And Zeke, for all his maturity, was only seventeen. Marianne worried about him, but she knew that even if things with his family never got better, she'd take him in. Or Rana. Or even Kevin, if it came down to it.

That was the thing she loved about Swanley. Everybody had someone who loved them. Even people like the Leventis—people knew them and had cared for them once. She was glad Luke had been knocked from his position, all of his properties under investigation as he waited for his bail hearing, but she still wondered what Simon had been like as a kid, as the best friend her father had trusted so much. Had all of it changed after Josie? Or had it been a slower change, one that her father missed through all Simon's familiar charm? Had the loss of his girlfriend turned him into someone willing to take advantage of his oldest friend, or had he been that way all along?

Janie emerged from the crowd, eyes searching, and lit up when she spotted Marianne. "Mom!" she called. "Come dance with me." Her eyes flicked to Rana and to their joined hands. "Bring your friend!"

"Want to come dance with my daughter and I?" asked Marianne.

Rana smiled. "I would love to."

Marianne let Janie's joy tug them both back into the fray, laughing as she followed.

They danced for three songs, jumping and swaying in a way she hadn't since at least the nineties, and as the music switched to a slower song, Marianne slid back out of the crowd to catch her breath. Rana had the same idea, it seemed, and both women made their way by silent agreement to the stand of maple trees just out of the brightly lit party.

The music was quieter here, out of the direct line of the speakers. Marianne and Rana stood alone on the grass, the streetlights dim in the distance, the Milky Way almost too bright above them in the clear night sky. They stood in silence for a moment, looking up at the stars.

"What are you going to do now?" asked Marianne, finally. "The restaurant is yours if you want to stay."

"I'm not sure," said Rana. "After all this, I might try to find my own building." She smiled. "Not that I don't trust you as a landlord. I think I want to own my own place."

"Oh," said Marianne. She wasn't sure what else to say.

"I was looking at a building over on Chestnut," said Rana.

"Chestnut Street? In Swanley?"

Rana looked at Marianne like she had two heads. "Yes, in Swanley. Where else?"

"I thought you said—I thought you meant you were leaving. That this town had been too much trouble."

Rana stepped closer and took both Marianne's hands in hers, her soft, warm skin smooth against Marianne's fingers. "I want to stay," she said. "I thought there might be some awkwardness if you became my landlord permanently. I'd rather we be friends. I'd like to stay in Swanley if you'll have me."

"Me, as a representative of the town, or me, Marianne?"

Rana leaned closer, until her lips brushed Marianne's jaw in a whisper below her ear. Marianne shivered. "You, Marianne Windmere. Do you want me to stay?"

"Yes," whispered Marianne. "Please. Stay." Marianne felt Rana's lips curve into a smile against her skin and their warmth spread through her.

Rana's hands dropped hers, sliding to curl around Marianne's waist, warm and inviting and familiar to Marianne despite only being this close to her for one night months ago. She reached up and wove her own fingers into Rana's thick, wavy hair, one hand cupping her cheek while the other curved around the back of Rana's neck. She pulled her head back slightly until she could press her nose into the hollow below Rana's jawline, the soft skin smelling of pie and cumin and warmth. Her lips brushed Rana's neck at her pulse, feeling the beating quicken beneath thin skin.

"Do you want this?" whispered Rana, her voice barely audible—if Marianne had been more than millimeters away, she wouldn't have heard her.

"What is this?" she whispered back, kissing her throat again as a warm spring breeze blew across the park.

"I don't know," said Rana. "But I think I like it."

Marianne hesitated. "I'm not sure what I want," Marianne said. "I don't really want sex most of the time."

"That's not what I want from you," Rana said into her ear, the words a low rustle. "It's you I want, not what you can do for me." She gave a little laugh. "Though you've done plenty for me already."

"You know, my apartment's just around the corner." Marianne pressed a kiss to the flat of Rana's cheekbone, feeling Rana's eyelashes fluttering against her skin. "We could go there if you'd like. It's a nice place."

"I hear the neighbor is a real pain," said Rana, tipping her head back up until her lips barely brushed Marianne's. "Very nosy."

Marianne grinned against Rana's mouth. "I think I can handle her."

"Then, yes," said Rana. "I'd love to."

Marianne pulled away, missing Rana's warmth against her instantly and wrapped her fingers around Rana's, pulling her back across the street to the bakery. They slipped in the side door so they wouldn't have to cut through the store and hurried up the steps to her warm dark apartment. In the living room, Marianne flicked on a lamp and turned to face Rana, taking a moment to just study her in the light.

Rana shifted under the scrutiny, a blush rising in her cheeks, her eyes flicking from Marianne's face down across her body and back up.

The easy, dreamy feel of their touches in the park had faded, leaving her the slightest bit anxious as she stood steps from where they'd fallen asleep together on that long ago, snowy night.

"Hi," she said, feeling a little silly. She was a grown woman who'd been married for nearly thirty years and given birth to three children. She was a business owner running her own bakery. And she'd just managed to overthrow the self-appointed dictator of a small town. How could she be so terrified of this gorgeous woman in front of her?

"Hi," said Rana. "Can I kiss you?"

"Yes," said Marianne, her nervousness melting away as Rana stepped toward her and pressed her soft, full lips to Marianne's.

*

By the time they made it back to the festivities around ten o'clock, the party had wound down, most of the celebrants wandering home while Marianne and Rana had disappeared to the bakery. Marianne, Ray, Zeke, and Rana were among the stragglers, picking up stray ribbons, lost napkins, and the occasional coat that had been tossed aside and forgotten. With the fire finally down to the barest embers, only the dim glow of the streetlights around the park lit their work.

"I'm going to give Mr. Mitchell here a ride home," said Ray, yawning. Zeke followed behind him, arms weighed down by folding chairs borrowed from Ray's, frankly astonishing, stash of patio furniture. "Rana, would you like to come along? I'll drop you on my way, if you'd like."

"It's not too far, thank you," said Rana. She glanced toward Marianne, meeting Marianne's eyes for a moment. Something warm and sweet glimmered in her gaze, and Marianne felt her face warming. "I can walk."

"Are you sure?"

"I'm sure." Rana stretched up and hugged Ray, kissed Zeke's cheek, and returned to picking up scattered paper plates from the grass.

Marianne watched the exchange with a smile, adding her tied bag of trash to the small pile they'd gathered in one corner of the park. In the morning, Michi would be by with the public works truck to pick the trash all up and take it to the dump. She could leave it there for one night, as much as it pained her to abandon the garbage like that.

Ray shook Marianne's hand as he passed, saying, "You did good," in her ear on his way by. She smiled at him and then returned Zeke's one-armed hug.

"Good party," he told her with a smile.

"Opening late tomorrow," she reminded him. "I'll see you at ten."

He gave her a thumbs-up and followed Ray to his truck, packing the chairs in the bed.

As the two of them slammed the doors to the truck, a hand landed on Marianne's shoulder. She turned slightly to see Rana beside her, cheeks pink in the low light and rapidly cooling wind. "Are you ready to go?" Rana asked her.

Marianne reached out a tentative hand, curling her fingers around Rana's own.

Chapter Twenty-Two

The bell above the door jingled and Marianne looked up, smiling at the young couple as they oohed and aahed over the display case.

"This town is so cute," gushed the taller, more femme girl, eyeing a turnover. "The lady at the shawarma shop was right—these look amazing."

Her shorter, more goth counterpart smiled at Marianne. "I'll take one of those apple muffins."

Marianne pulled the muffin out and bagged it along with the other girl's mini pumpkin pie. "You had lunch at the Cairo Cafe?"

The tall one nodded. "That falafel was so good." She paused. "Wait, should I not talk about that place while I'm buying stuff here?"

The door opened again as Marianne laughed, and Rana shut it gently behind herself. The girls both turned to look at her and then turned back to Marianne, twin looks of confusion spreading over their faces.

"I'm glad you liked your lunch," said Rana, cheeks flushed from the brisk walk down the block.

She wasn't in Marianne's building anymore; instead, in the next building over in a space better suited to her business. She'd even hired two of Zeke's friends to help out, and they were finally competent enough to be left alone. The space she'd vacated next door was under renovation with a contract in place for a frozen yogurt place set to open in July.

Rana waved at Zeke in the corner before kissing Marianne on the cheek. "Hello, love. The work next door looks wonderful." She handed Marianne a foil-wrapped pita. "I left the last few customers with Stevie and Mahshid, but I brought you the end of the basturma. Do you mind if I stay here and do my budgets?" She held up her computer bag.

"You're just angling for another slice of pie," said Marianne, already cutting the slice of cherry as Zeke took drink orders and then poured the girls two coffees.

"A *lesbian bakery!*" whispered the small goth to her partner. "Oh my god, we *have* to move here."

"Bisexual bakery, actually," said Rana.

"All around queer," Zeke agreed.

Marianne laughed.

Both girls grinned. "Even better!" The tall one paid for both pastries and then followed her partner out, whispering animatedly.

"I'm out," called Zeke as he untied his apron. "I have class in an hour, and I have to finish the reading. Jamie should be here in an hour or so."

"Rinse the muffin tins before you go, and I won't tell Joe you didn't do your homework." Marianne wagged a finger at him. "At least not this time." She glanced at the clock. She couldn't quite leave her new employee, Charlie, Carol's brother's grandchild, alone in the store yet, but they and Zeke had been running the store without her every Tuesday for the last month. Zeke had taken on responsibility for training them, and Marianne had known he'd be a fantastic teacher. The two of them behind the counter together, laughing and serving customers and handling the business as well as she or her father could have warmed her to her core. She hadn't realized how hard she'd been running herself with her seventy-hour weeks and no life outside the bakery until she'd suddenly had an extra fifteen hours a week.

"You drive a hard bargain," replied Zeke. "But all right, fine. I'll see you tomorrow, guys." He grinned suddenly. "I'll bring a pride flag by if that's what's going to sell muffins." He pushed through the doors into the kitchen, whistling.

"You know, my daughter says the young gay kids are looking for new places to shop," said Rana speculatively. "Maybe that's your niche."

Marianne grabbed her wrist and pulled her close, pressing her face into Rana's sweet-smelling hair. "I could live with that," she said. "And now they've even got a place to park."

Rana pulled back just enough to look her in the face, her expression turning serious. "There's a problem there."

"There is?"

"I think we need more bike racks if that's the crowd we're hoping to win."

"We can do that."

"And I was thinking," continued Rana. "A collaboration? I think I could make something wonderful with your bread and my meats. Shawarma croissants?"

"I think that sounds delicious," said Marianne. She laughed. She had hopes for the future, plans for expanding the bakery, and a vision of retirement someday. She even had a secret hope, one that seemed more realistic every day: that in ten years or so, she would wander into the bakery as a customer and let Zeke pamper her. She hadn't quite gotten up the nerve to ask him yet, but she thought he might like the idea, too, once he finished his degree.

Rana smiled at her, dimples framing her smile. "What's so funny?" she asked.

"I'm happy." Marianne pulled Rana close, kissing her cheek. "I didn't expect it."

"The best things aren't expected," said Rana. "You should know that by now."

"I guess I do." Marianne let herself laugh, enjoying the warmth of the bakery, and Rana, and the easy shape of her life.

Acknowledgements

This book wouldn't have been possible without my community of writers and friends and family. A first thanks as always to Mike, partner extraordinaire, who read this book many many times over the last two years and made it better every time.

To my writing group: Felicia Davin and Kristin Collins for letting me text them constantly with plot holes (and helping to shovel content into them!); Courtney Collins for fixing all my legal issues and using her law degree for good; Jeff Hudecek for scrubbing the heck out of my first few chapters and making them shine; Wren Wallis and Brian White and all the other Panera writers for being badass writing buddies and eating so much soup with me. We all deserve whiskey and stickers.

To my parents, who are the world's best cheerleaders and who believe I'll be a bestseller soon.

To my first readers Tasha Nova Costa and Baize White (we miss you, Baize, and may you rest in power and peace always) for beautiful suggestions and spotting all the issues before my poor editor had to.

To my brother Patrick and all my lawyer customers at my post office, for letting me badger them with questions about obscure property law.

And to AO3 and the OTW, where I learned to write.

About the Author

Valentine lives in Boston with her partner and child. She mails things all day and writes all night.

Her life's ambition is to eat the cuisine of every single country.

Twitter: @ghostalservice

Other books by this author

"Loose in the Heel, Tight in the Toe" within *Once Upon a Rainbow, Volume Three*
"Piece of Cake" within *Teacher's Pet, Volume One*
"Dead Letter" within *Into the Mystic, Volume Two*
Checked Baggage: A Thanksgiving Romance
Surface Tension